THE KILL DOG

Maggie is in Prague on a Market Research project. But when a Russian tank rolls up outside her hotel, dashing all her plans, she decides to face the country's menacing and violent situation and drive towards the border. On the way, she acquires a passenger — a fugitive. Jan is a Czech archaeologist, carrying a valuable secret, ignorant of its significance or value. But when he eventually faces his enemies in Czechoslovakia, events prove more dramatic than he'd ever anticipated.

Books by John Burke
in the Linford Mystery Library:

THE GOLDEN HORNS
THE POISON CUPBOARD
THE DARK GATEWAY
FEAR BY INSTALMENTS
MURDER, MYSTERY AND MAGIC
ONLY THE RUTHLESS CAN PLAY

JOHN BURKE

THE KILL DOG

Complete and Unabridged

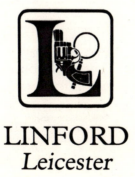

LINFORD
Leicester

First published in Great Britain

First Linford Edition
published 2012

British Library CIP Data

Burke, John Frederick, *1922 –*
 The kill dog.- -(Linford mystery library)
 1. Suspense fiction.
 2. Large type books.
 I. Title II. Series
 823.9'14–dc23

ISBN 978–1–4448–1364–7

Published by
F. A. Thorpe (Publishing)
Anstey, Leicestershire

Set by Words & Graphics Ltd.
Anstey, Leicestershire
Printed and bound in Great Britain by
T. J. International Ltd., Padstow, Cornwall

This book is printed on acid-free paper

Truth will prevail.

— JAN HUS (1415)

No, truth does not prevail, it keeps being vanquished; but it has a strange gift of invincibility — it survives.

— IVAN KLIMA (1968)

1

The hotel was stuffy and old-fashioned but comfortable. With the double windows closed the rooms were quiet, apart from an occasional abdominal rumbling deep in the heating system. Unfortunately there was no way of controlling this heat within each room. Either you lay awake gasping for breath or you opened the windows and still lay awake, jolted by the intermittent roar and thump of traffic.

Maggie Armitage had an inside room overlooking the well of the building. At least the squeal of the trams was muffled here; but to make up for this there was the rasp of an extractor fan three floors down, shrilling as though it had not been lubricated since the last days of the Austro-Hungarian Empire. On her first night she had achieved only three hours' sleep. Tonight, exhausted after tramping along streets and in and out of shops all over the city, she had hoped to succumb immediately and wake ready for a determined attack next morning.

She turned over, mumbling to herself. Drowsy thoughts transformed themselves into halting German and then into gibberish. In a waking dream she walked again into that cosmetics shop and tried to believe that eventually they would understand what she was trying to put over to them. So polite, so friendly; but so baffled.

Perhaps tomorrow she ought to go back to that nice man in Pragoexport and listen a bit more respectfully to his advice.

Mrs Chinnery wouldn't approve.

Maggie shoved her head into her hard, square, flat pillow.

'Stay away from the jacks in office,' Mrs Chinnery had exhorted her. 'They'll only tell you what they want you to hear. Propaganda and generalisations. No help at all. Talk to the people who really do the job. People like that are the same everywhere — real people, I mean.'

Real people. Everywhere the same. Maggie started to argue with Mrs Chinnery but found that Mrs Chinnery had marched briskly away and was crossing the road towards Marks & Spencer's (and what was Marks & Sparks doing *here*, for goodness' sake?) and a tram was bearing down on her. Maggie gasped and stepped off the pavement. It was steeper than she had anticipated. Her foot plunged down, a shock struck up her spine, and she twisted round at an awkward angle and found herself half upright in bed, her heart pounding.

'Marks 'n' no smoking an' that's why, that's it,' she heard herself mutter. One of those philosophical discoveries made only as you fumble into wakefulness.

The rumble of the approaching tram seemed to go on, too, in her head. The window panes trembled. Didn't the traffic in this place ever stop? There was a heavy pounding close at hand, then some distant thuds as though blasting were going on through the night in the quarries outside the city.

Maggie turned over once more. The noise died away. Then it came back, like a convoy of lorries thundering in from another direction. It was as bad as trying to sleep near Covent Garden Market.

In spite of the oppressiveness of the hot, still air she stumbled out of bed and closed the window. She felt utterly weary as she slumped down again, but still tossed about in a sleepless haze.

Somewhere in the hotel, voices rose in what sounded like an argument. Or maybe it was just that the language always sounded like that anyway. Footsteps ran down a staircase.

At last she slept. Her dreams were noisy and complicated.

In the morning she felt sticky. She rang the bell for a maid to come and unlock the bathroom. After five minutes she rang again. Nobody appeared. Nobody moved on the landing.

Maggie gave herself a quick, impatient all-over wash and went down to breakfast.

The room used for breakfast opened out of the entrance hall, immediately flanking the main doors. In the evening it tempted passers-by in from the street for wine, beer, coffee and snacks. Maggie went past a group of men arguing heatedly at the reception desk, and down the two steps to the entrance. In the breakfast-room nobody was eating. Three or four people stood by the windows staring out through the yellowing lace curtains.

Straight ahead of Maggie were the main doors. Neatly framed in the large glass panels was a tank, its gun jutting across the street towards her.

Instinctively Maggie stepped back, jarring her heel against the lower step.

The men at the desk broke up and moved away. Maggie turned and approached the desk from one side, keeping out of the direct line of fire.

The harassed-looking clerk began talking urgently. She slowed him down by breaking into her laboured but adequate German, reminding him that she didn't understand Czech.

He gulped, and then said simply:
'The Russians. We are invaded.'
Russians?

It was absurd. Invasions happened only in distant trouble-spots, in far corners of the world; never in places where you yourself were likely to be.

Yet here she was, and out there was that tank: here in Prague, on the 21st of August 1968.

*　*　*

Well, this put paid to Mrs Chinnery's schemes for expansion into Eastern Europe.

'We're going to put silk drapes where the iron curtain used to be.' It sounded fine and symbolic when you talked about it in London. Mrs Chinnery was still, cosily, in London. Maggie wasn't.

She stood back as other hotel guests came down the stairs and clustered round the desk. They all had lots of questions, but nobody had any answers.

Through the breakfast-room door there was a flicker of movement. A solitary waiter, perhaps living on the premises, was gallantly laying out plates of rolls and butter. Maggie went in and had a fruit juice and coffee. From where she sat she could see people moving along the street. They were neither aggressive nor cautious. Young men stooped under the barrel of the gun as if it were no more than a temporary traffic hazard. Others stood back and gazed blankly at it.

Maggie left her breakfast chit on the table and went to the main doors. A young soldier squatting on top of the tank stared impassively back at her.

She put a hand on the door, hesitated and then walked out. The Russian's eyes and the dark mouth of the gun were still focused on her.

A middle-aged woman bumped into her. They both said 'Pardon' with firm, loud politeness, demonstrating some sort of mystical solidarity.

Another tank guarded the corner of the street. Three girls, arm in arm, made faces at it as they passed. A Russian soldier in a grubby black leather jacket unslung his tommy-gun. Maggie felt a terrible urge to turn back to the hotel and shut herself away in the lavatory. Instead, she walked on.

In a wide main street a car was squashed against the kerb, mangled as though a giant foot had stamped down on it.

Maggie shivered, thinking of her own

car in the hotel garage. Would she ever be allowed to drive it out, now? What happened during an invasion: martial law, commandeering of all cars, arrest of all Western infiltrators . . . ?

Ridiculous.

Yet no more ridiculous, no more incredible than these obscene grey slugs fouling every street.

The shops were shut. There were no trams or buses. It could almost have been a national holiday, with people sauntering down the middle of the road, looking around in wonderment.

'First in the East,' had been one of Mrs Chinnery's slogans. 'Pre-Sales Research where it's really needed.'

They wouldn't be needing it now, by the look of it. She'd have to stick to the Midlands and the Home Counties.

In the distance there was a rattling noise which might have been firing. Two young men turned in that direction and hurried away with terrifying eagerness. Did they really want to be killed?

An armoured car clattered across a junction.

There was a smell of burning oil. Smoke drifted down a side street. Maggie looked along the grey chasm between peeling, ragged walls, and saw flame belching from the top of a tank.

She had always known that she was not the stuff of which heroines are made. She returned to the hotel, carefully not making any gesture which the watchful tank might construe as provocative, and went indoors. She asked what news there was and when she would be able to get back to London.

There was no news. Only rumour. It was not until the afternoon that details began to filter through. People came in, chattered, and went out again. The lift operator sat hunched over a transistor radio, often surrounded by five or six hotel guests.

Dubcek had been seized and taken away by the Russians. Cernik was gone, nobody knew where. They had been executed already. No, they were in captivity and would be executed as soon as a puppet government had been formed. Svoboda was going to broadcast any minute now ... Svoboda was a prisoner in the castle and would not be allowed to broadcast ...

'Keep calm.'

Calm?

The Russians had occupied the airport and it was said that they had sealed the frontiers. They were everywhere, squatting on their tanks, waiting. It was inconceivable that they should just go on sitting there like that. The lull wouldn't last. Soon there would be more than those bursts of sporadic firing.

An Englishman who had been attending a geological congress hammered the desk.

'We were invited here officially. It's up to someone to get us out.'

The clerk's faltering English wasn't good enough for the geologist, and he appealed to Maggie. 'You're English?' said the man, and spent the next fifteen minutes complaining about the injustice of it all. For years they had been planning this international conference in Prague, and they'd hardly started and now this had happened.

At first she had half welcomed the presence of a fellow-countryman. Now she was glad to find an excuse for edging away from him.

She tried to ring the British Embassy. Others were trying to do the same thing, and it was impossible to get through.

That night there was a curfew. Hotels and restaurants were closed. One might have thought that a plague was raging. Perhaps there soon would be — or at any rate a famine. If no food were allowed in . . . if they were to be starved into submission while the Russians rampaged through the city and the countryside . . .

But in the morning there were even more people in the streets. Bursts of gun-fire resounded from Wenceslas Square. Radios babbled on, while Maggie tried to get translations from listeners who wanted only to go on listening and then to argue among themselves.

A crackle of words, a snarl, the quick turning of the knob.

'They say,' explained one man, 'we must find a new way of behaving. We citizens. We go on with the normal life, peaceful, we ignore the invaders.'

'Fascists,' said the clerk at the desk, over and over again to anyone who asked him anything whatsoever. 'Fascists.'

On Friday he beckoned to Maggie. 'We hear the Austrian frontier is open. Some special train may go through Germany also — today, tomorrow, we do not know. But by road, Austria is safer.'

At last she was able to get through to the Embassy.

'Austria?' said the tired but helpful voice in the receiver. 'Mm. Yes, we're getting a football team out by coach' — he made it sound reassuringly, humorously like a game which didn't have to become too earnest — 'but that doesn't mean it's all clear for anyone else. Lot of Russian stuff on the roads down there. Wait until the situation clarifies, if I were you.'

She waited until Sunday, conscious all the time of the alternating bouts of optimism and despair all round her.

Dubcek was alive. He was in Moscow, negotiating. Svoboda was there. Cernik was there. They would be coming back on

12

Sunday night. Or Monday.

They were standing firm.

They would have done a deal.

The country would not yield.

The Russians were going to close all roads in and out of Prague from Sunday night onwards. Foreigners should get out, and then crossing-points on the borders would be sealed off once and for all.

Again Maggie rang the Embassy.

'Well, yes, maybe it would be as well to get moving. Our people seem to be getting out all right at the moment.'

Maggie threw her case into the Renault and got moving.

★ ★ ★

There was more traffic about now. Was it really possible that after such a brutal blow a city could get back to normal, could pretend there was nobody there and nothing wrong? Trams were running, and a few buses. Private cars edged tentatively past the brooding tanks.

She found her way out of the dusty streets with some difficulty but at last struck the southbound Highway 3, following the line of the river towards the low, smoky hills. She wanted to look back and make some sentimental farewell gesture; but she had hardly got to know Prague, it meant little more than a congestion of old streets and crumbling façades, scaffolding and holes in the road. Sorry, Mrs Chinnery, but we'll have to write that one off: no sheer nylon nighties, no depilatories, deodorants, dandruff destroyers or pantie stockings for the downtrodden East. Western Decadence will have to stay right where it is.

Once she was clear of Prague, the road was almost deserted. She flinched when she saw a battery of anti-aircraft guns thrusting up into the sky. She hoped they couldn't be swung down at an angle low enough to blast her off the face of the earth.

A tank sat in a side road as though waiting for nonexistent traffic-lights to change. She drove on and nobody challenged, nobody fired after her. Still there was that sense of waiting — of a contrived lull during which aliens like herself could scuttle out and get far away before the whips came out and the jackboots came down.

At a fork in the road she slowed, looking for a signpost. There must have been one here, but it had been torn down. She stopped and studied her map. The main road ahead must be the one for Benesov.

After a while it narrowed and wound its way through a straggling village of dull yellow and ochre houses, emerging on to a crossroads with a decrepit iron Crucifixion in the centre like a lopsided traffic beacon. Ahead of Maggie, a grey Skoda was drawn up by the roadside, half obscured from her view by a Russian tank. She slowed and swerved in to the side of the road before reaching the junction. There was something threatening in the tableau: the stationary tank, the man in uniform standing on the grass beside the ditch and talking to a civilian who was probably the owner of the Skoda. She sat quite still and hoped, with frank cowardice, that whatever was going to happen would be over and done with before she had to drive past.

The car quivered gently beneath her as three more tanks lumbered in from the road on the right. The leader made a wide swing round the stationary tank on the corner. Maggie saw what was bound to happen. It worked itself out in slow motion, with all the rhythmic absurdity of an old silent film. The tank clattered into the middle of the road, spun on its tracks to make a tighter turn and caught the parked car behind its offside rear wing. The Russian by the ditch stepped hastily to one side. The civilian made an instinctive move towards his car and then dodged as it rose several feet in the air, came to a grinding halt against a boulder and slid slowly down into the ditch.

The tank stopped like a dog surprised by its own strength, waiting for an admonishment. Then it nosed out into the road again, and resumed its way with its two followers clanking along behind.

The Russian on the grass laughed and slapped the civilian matily on the arm. Then he climbed back into the stationary tank, which lurched off after its fellows.

Like a silent film, thought Maggie

again. You half expected Laurel and Hardy to climb out of the warped shape of the upended car.

She drove slowly over the crossroads and drew up beside the man. He turned at the sound of the car, tensed against another assault, another humiliation.

He must have been in his late thirties, with deep brown eyes and a dark, dour face. He was tall for a Czech, and his finely bony nose was quite alien to the characteristically broad, flattened Slav features.

Maggie wondered what the German for 'Can I give you a tow?' was, abandoned the idea, and said slowly and distinctly: 'Can I help you?'

He put his head on one side as though recognising a foreign intonation in her German. Then in quiet, uninflected English he said: 'I am on my way to Linz. No . . . I was on my way to Linz. And then England.'

'You're not English?'

'No, I am Czech. But I think there is no room for me here any more.' He looked ruefully down at the car in the ditch. 'Perhaps I should have left yesterday. Or waited until tomorrow. Or I should have reached here half an hour sooner, or half an hour later.'

'Have you got any rope in your car? I could try pulling you out.'

He shook his head. 'It is very twisted. I shall be surprised if it's in working order.'

Maggie drew up on to the grass verge and walked back with him to the wreck.

Seen this closely, the car did indeed look like a write-off. Its side had been crushed in over the rear engine, two windows were shattered, and even a breakdown truck would have had difficulty in getting a good purchase on it from this angle.

There was a faint snap. A rope lashing luggage to the roof grid came loose, and two cases slithered down behind the car.

Maggie said: 'Looks as though I'd better give you a lift.'

He shook his head again, not so much in refusal as in mockery of everything that fate had recently decreed. After a moment he looked back up the road in the direction of Prague.

A truck roared past them. A long-distance coach with a German or Austrian name along its side slowed at the crossroads as though to stop and offer help, then accelerated into a cloud of dust.

'Perhaps.' He seemed to be musing aloud. 'Or perhaps it would not be right.'

Maggie said brusquely: 'Is somebody after you?'

'After me?'

'Chasing you.'

'I . . . hope not.'

'But they might be?'

'Since Wednesday, everything is possible. Everything,' he said wryly, 'except sanity.'

'We'd better start shifting that luggage of yours,' said Maggie.

2

Jan Melisek was a Professor in the Archaeological Institute of the Czechoslovak Academy of Sciences. This much he told the girl in answer to her polite, conventional questions as she drove through Benesov and on towards Tabor. He didn't want to tell her much else — it was not natural to talk too freely, for years it had not been natural to talk freely in this country even to friends, let alone to strangers — but she was driving him to the border and he owed her the ordinary civilities of conversation. He hoped they could stick to generalities, even though they made no sense. None of it made any sense . . . save as a terrible parallel to what had been happening to him as one ordinary individual over these last months. Ordinary? What, at any time, had been ordinary?

He was still numbed. He still had no idea of how he would come out of it.

'What made them do it?' this Miss Armitage was asking. 'What could have possessed them?'

'Fear,' he said. 'Fear, and spite, and ignorance.'

'But the ill will they'll cause . . . '

He laughed. Her anger identified her as one of those good liberals who saw yet another hope crumbling. The erosion of ideals worked more swiftly than she had yet realised. 'Ill will?' he echoed. 'You think they have ever worried about concepts like that?'

'But they can't want a war. The fools. Why did they do it?' A good liberal, more savage at the destruction of ideas that ought to have worked than any experienced Middle European would ever be.

'There won't be a war,' he said.

'They can't just walk in . . . and nothing happen. Not today. Not after . . . well, after everything.'

'Nobody else wants to start a war just because of us. They haven't wanted to do that since the seventeenth century.'

Her slanted, slightly narrowed green eyes were concentrating on the road ahead; but he could tell that she was being just as attentive to him as to the route. The route was merely a matter of calculation: he was a person, a refugee from melodrama on whom she could whet her curiosity.

Abruptly she said: 'I wouldn't have thought *you* would have to leave. I mean, your kind of work — it's safe enough, surely?'

'Nothing has been safe.'

'But archaeology — that can't change, can it? It can't get political all of a sudden.'

'Anything can become political, if the authorities want it to be so.'

'It's crazy.'

'Yes.'

'But in your kind of work,' she persisted, 'how could there be any trouble? What difference does it make to Communists or Tories or Social Democrats or what-have-you whether a pot is a thousand years old or two thousand years old?'

'I was regarded as politically unreliable,' he said.

'How can an archaeologist be politically unreliable?'

'My mother was Welsh.'

The girl laughed. He had to join in. It was so absurd. Only an outsider could really enjoy the absurdity.

'That would go down well at home,' she said. ''I'm politically unreliable — my mother's Welsh.''

'She met my father during the First World War. I had an older brother. He was killed during the Second.'

'And your parents?'

'Both dead.' He added: 'They missed the worst.'

The undulating hills rolled away before them, the skyline broken by an occasional bulbous church tower or a saw-edge of pine forest. The farther mountains were no more than sullen clouds against the horizon. He glanced at the girl's profile — the soft but confident chin, gently smiling lips, lazy droop of her left eyebrow — and his affection for all things English went momentarily sour. Her smile was the smile of patient incredulity. She had seen the tanks and the soldiers, but she still didn't really believe that people could have lived, or half-lived, with that sort of threat on their doorstep for so long. The English . . . it was all too easy for them. That was what he most admired and most resented: the easy indifference of them, even when they seemed most indignant. They cherished their ignorance of danker political climates, of the shabbiness which was so much a part of everyday life all over Europe, of the virus of deceit and intellectual decay which ate remorselessly into the very spirit.

He wanted to shake the attractive Miss Armitage. He found he was saying more than he had meant to, in an effort to make her feel the hurt. And yet he was still incapable of telling her anything that mattered. What he said was clear and concise and true; but it was only as much of the truth as one would find on the surface. He might have been sketching in the configuration of a Bronze Age settlement, providing a simple outline which could do no more than hint at the complexity of fragments below — fragments which would need to be sifted painstakingly a thousand times before a recognisable pattern emerged.

★ ★ ★

Brok had brought the paper to him almost a year ago.

'I wonder if you would care to add your signature to this, my dear Melisek?'

'What is it?'

Brok laid the page of signatures in front of him. Discussion of the declaration he was supposed to sign was, apparently, unnecessary.

'We all feel it's time we spoke out,' said Brok.

Jan skimmed down the column of scrawled signatures. 'All?' he asked softly. Several names were missing.

'I'm just collecting the last few.'

'Are there some you tried to collect, and didn't get?'

'Some of our colleagues,' said Brok, 'take a perverse pleasure in being unco-operative. It's part of the very unhealthiness we're protesting about.'

Jan turned back the page to the

declaration itself.

It was in the form of an appeal to the President of the Republic to take strong action against disloyal writers and journalists who were undermining the dynamic development of true Czech culture by posturing and empty gestures. There was a danger of counter-revolutionary ideas spreading and of the democratic workers' community being enfeebled by the irresponsibility of deviationist individuals. The Communist Party's sensitive cultural policy and its scrupulousness in evaluating creative works arising as a result was in danger of contamination from revisionist writers, journalists and film-makers who sought only to subjectivise their own tendency towards alienation and nihilism. Scientists of the Czechoslovak Socialist Republic were distressed by this self-indulgent, disorienting exhibitionism, and promised the President and First Secretary their full support and patriotic enthusiasm in any measures he felt it necessary to undertake against reactionary groups or individuals who had so shamelessly proclaimed their hostility towards socialism.

Jan said: 'Turgid stuff. Who wrote it?'

'It's a communal effort.'

'Reads like it. Anyway, I don't agree.'

'It is so much more satisfactory if we all sign,' said Brok.

'Satisfactory to say that we none of us approve of writers who demand freedom from censorship, freedom to criticise obvious injustice, and freedom to tell certain people they're illiterate and incompetent?'

'Destructive criticism is undermining the nation.'

'A bulldozer would do the job more quickly. I'll go that far. Then we could start rebuilding from scratch. In the meantime, I don't feel inclined to blame the writers for saying what we all feel.'

'I'm sorry you take this attitude.' But Brok was not at all sorry. His teeth were bared momentarily in a yellow grin. He relished this further proof that Professor Melisek was a disruptive element. But nobody would ever be able to reproach him for not doing his best. 'All you have to do,' he coaxed, 'is sign.'

'I have no intention of signing.'

'It will arouse comment.'

'I'm all in favour of comment — of any kind.'

'Of any kind?' said Brok. 'You think it right that the work of scientists, historians, scholars like ourselves should be disrupted by subjectivist word-jugglers who want to shatter the fabric of society? Men with no academic standards, no training to speak of. Writers . . . ' Author of a vast ethnographical treatise on the Slavs of Central Europe which was required University reading — without which compulsion it would certainly have been declared unreadable by any responsible critic — Brok could nevertheless spit out the word 'Writer' as venomously as though any man who put pen to paper must be regarded as a plague-spot on the body politic.

Jan said: 'If we turn on each other, heaven knows where we'll all end up.'

'Things are getting out of hand.'

'Out of whose hand?'

Brok prodded the list of signatures an inch forward, offering one last chance. 'You won't sign?'

'No.'

Brok took the paper away.

Jan did not mention the matter to Blanka when he got home, but by the next evening she knew. A hushed report had been passed on to her by the wife of one of Jan's colleagues, a timid expert on ninth-century Moravia whose name had appeared very high up on Brok's list.

'So you've done it again!' was Blanka's greeting.

He had been following up an elusive lead in the library at Strahov, and had walked home through the castle. The late summer haze lay like rose-tinted smoke along the river. The raggedly packed houses of the Little Quarter tumbled precipitously down the slope, eddied round the bulk of St Nicholas's Church, and spilled onwards. However often you walked this way, you never saw the same picture twice; light and colour never repeated themselves.

Enjoying the smell and shimmer and warmth of the afternoon, Jan crossed the Powder Bridge and went at a leisurely pace down the hill. Theories were still being slotted into place in his mind when he opened the door of the flat and had Blanka's welcome flung at him.

He kissed her. It was a ritual observance which she expected even when she was preparing a quarrel.

'Sorry I'm late.' He couldn't imagine any other reason for her anger. 'I wanted to think some things out.'

'I'm not surprised. And I only hope you've changed your mind.'

Reluctantly he abandoned his mental quest for the relevance of that vague literary inference, and tried to readjust. 'Changed my mind?'

'This business of signing Brok's list.'

'How do you know about that?'

'Mrs Jasik told me.'

'Ah. I see.'

'Well?'

'I haven't given it another thought.'

'You're determined to lose your job? You really don't care if we starve?'

'I hardly think it'll come to that.'

'You hardly think it'll come to that,' she cried derisively. 'It's happened before, hasn't it? To people like . . . well . . . ' Her voice swooped half an octave. Even after all this time she didn't like to name names. None of them did. Not too loudly, anyway. She said: 'You know very well what it was like.'

'That was ten years ago.'

Ten years since the Czechoslovak Academy of Sciences had been subjected to a Class and Political Verification Procedure decreed by the Political Bureau of the Central Committee. A fifth of those examined had been expelled, demoted or reprimanded. Since then most of the staff had been very cautious. Conformity paid better dividends than originality.

'It could happen again,' said Blanka.

A faint sputtering from the gas cooker distracted her. As she turned to it and reached for another pan, slamming it down on one of the burners, Jan opened the sideboard drawer and began to take out knives and forks.

Over her shoulder Blanka said: 'Jasik hasn't got half your ability. Not a quarter. Everybody knows that. But he'll get advancement — he'll get a good administrative job long before you will.'

'But I don't want an administrative job.'

It was true, of course, that Jasik was tidy and sensible in his thinking. Slavonic studies were rated more highly than Celtic studies. Typical of Jan, said Blanka's hostile back, to have chosen Celtic research just at a time when it was frowned on. The preaching of Pan-Slav doctrines was the official line. It could hardly be denied that the very name of Bohemia derived from a Celtic tribe, but such studies ought not to be pursued with too great a zeal. 'Just because your mother was Welsh . . . ' Blanka wasn't growling it out loud at this moment, but she had done so often enough.

They sat at the table and for a few minutes ate without speaking. Blanka in the kitchen was noisy, dropping things and cursing at the drudgery and slamming irascibly about as though determined to ruin every meal she prepared; but in fact she was a good cook, and this evening her pork and dumplings were, as usual, delicious.

Jan said as much. 'Delicious.'

She took this as a signal to renew hostilities.

'If you go on the way you are doing,' she said, 'we'll soon be out of here. They'll pass the flat on to someone who toes the line.'

It was a long time since she had seemed to aim for a head-on collision. Recently they had been, if not tranquil, at least indifferent.

Jan made a mistake. He knew it was a mistake even as he was making it. Trying to reason with her, trying to establish facts from which everything else must follow — and which could hardly fail to infuriate Blanka — he said: 'Look . . . you know what my views are. You've always known.'

'Selfish,' she said. 'I know that much.'

'I was honest with you when we were married. I haven't changed — '

'Stubborn,' she picked him up at once. 'That's what you are: stubborn, and proud of it. Other people change. Why not you?'

'I warned you of the difficulties. I told you I'd never make concessions to this system. We agreed — '

'I didn't know it would be as bad as this.'

'As this?'

He pushed his chair back from the table and looked round the room, challenging her to do the same.

They were better off than many, and she was well aware of it. They had their own entrance hall, now split up to accommodate a narrow bathroom, and they had two rooms — kitchen and sitting-room. There was space in the kitchen here for one bed along the wall, where Blanka slept so that he could have the small sitting-room to himself when he wanted to work late. Several times he had offered to change over, but she preferred the kitchen, particularly when they were quarrelling: it gave her the moral satisfaction of being self-sacrificing.

Some married couples had to share two rooms like this with ageing parents, or with children. Some, downgraded because of purges in the Fifties, could not afford any of the tidy luxuries which the Mel-iseks enjoyed. Privacy was a rarity, especially where there were children.

Here, in this flat, there were no elderly relations grumbling about the better times in the past when a man could do an honest job and food didn't cost the earth . . . on and on, inescapable because there was no other room to escape to. No elderly relations. And no children.

Once Jan had wondered if children would have made a difference to Blanka and himself. Now he had given up wondering.

There was the faint, far squeal of a tram slowing down the hill towards the square.

Blanka said: 'Can't you tell things are going to tighten up again? Can't you feel it? It's all been too easy just lately.'

'Then we'll have to go on just as we did before.'

'Nobody else makes silly gestures. Nobody else has to be so high and mighty.'

'Not everybody signed that disgusting rubbish.'

'Your bright young friend Adamec, for example? Don't tell me *he* didn't sign?'

'He didn't.'

'That close to Brok and he refused? I don't believe it.'

'When I saw the list — '

'Ah. When you saw the list. But don't tell me Brok saved you for the end. Don't tell me there weren't others who signed later.'

'A few, maybe. Plenty who didn't. And not Lada.'

'Ask him.'

'I don't need to.'

Blanka got up and began to clear the table. She clattered the dishes into the sink as though daring them to break.

'You don't *want* to,' she said. She jerked her head towards the door of the sitting-room. 'Go and phone him.'

He had no intention of telephoning Ladislav and asking bluntly whether he had surrendered to Brok. But the thought of seeing the younger man, talking, relaxing, was an inviting one.

'Phone him,' Blanka repeated.

'I might go and have a drink with him.'

'Do. Do go and have a drink with him. And ask him. And when you get back, tell me the truth.'

Jan got up and stood quite still. Blanka turned back from the sink, flushed, and leaned for a moment on the table.

'No,' she said. 'I'm sorry.' The words were dragged out of her. 'You always tell the truth. I know that.' Her mouth twisted as though to declare that this made things, if anything, worse.

Jan telephoned Ladislav Adamec and arranged to meet him at their usual place: not quite halfway — ten minutes' walk for Jan, fifteen for Ladislav.

★ ★ ★

Jan climbed the hill and went into the kavarna on the corner. Ladislav had just arrived: he must have walked briskly up from the Little Quarter. He was ordering a coffee and a mineral water. Jan asked for a beer. They nodded companionably at each other, and sat silent for a minute or two.

Jan looked forward to these casual, undemanding meetings, away from the Institute. They never planned earnest debate. They didn't play chess. They simply met and chatted, and drifted off home when they felt like it. If the conversation failed to catch fire, they abandoned it. If they didn't meet for a couple of weeks, neither felt peevish or neglected.

Ladislav Adamec was ten years younger than Jan. He looked pale and boyish, and had a slight hesitation in his speech: not so much a stammer as an occasional uncertainty when you felt he was afraid of taking the plunge and committing himself. It might have been this shy hesitancy which had commended itself to Brok and secured the young man a post under the Director himself. But behind the pallor, young Adamec had clear-cut opinions of his own on Slavonic studies and on administration in general. The tremor of his lips as he prepared to speak was as likely to result in a decisive outburst as in the nervous deference Brok would have preferred.

Jan said: 'Haven't seen you about for a day or two.'

'I've been down at the publisher's.'

'Oh, the encyclopaedia.'

'Yes.' Ladislav grimaced. 'The encyclopaedia.'

'Headaches?'

'And delays. Most of today I was just sitting and waiting for corrected galleys. Nobody's fault, of course.'

They both grinned, and drank. Delays and incompetence were never anybody's fault. When there was blame, it had to be directed against crypto-bourgeois pressures exerted from West Germany or the will-sapping contamination of Radio Free Europe. Never against the true workers.

'There were four of us there, waiting,' said Ladislav. 'Their senior editor and two others I hadn't met before. We sat around and talked. Funny — it turned out they'd all three of them been in labour camps. Or camps of one kind and another. One of them under the Nazis, one under . . . ' He glanced round the smoky room and then said defiantly: 'Under this lot. And the third under both.'

Jan finished his beer. The story was familiar and depressing. Ironical, pitiful; but in this century there hadn't been much pity to spare.

All he could do was shrug and add his own footnote.

'I did my military service down the

mines. One of the last — I had an extra year, and then they closed down the camps and pretended they hadn't existed. I wasn't considered worthy of being in the army. Or perhaps they didn't trust me with a rifle.'

He waved to the waiter, who passed three times before acknowledging the summons and bringing another bottle.

'So.' Ladislav gulped. 'S-so . . . if you are honest and harmless, then — '

'Nobody who's honest is harmless.'

'That makes our revered Director the innocent of all time.'

Jan had not meant to ask, but found himself seizing the opportunity. 'If you've been away this last couple of days, you won't have seen the manifesto?'

'Oh . . . oh, yes.' A word rustled like spit on Ladislav's lip. 'Th . . . that. Yes, I've seen it.'

'When?'

Over his coffee cup Ladislav smiled a wearily adult smile that didn't belong on his unmarked face. 'Before it reached you. Did you think it was later — and that I had signed?'

'I wouldn't have blamed you.'

'No?'

'It's so much easier to go along with them. Simpler.'

'They make me sick.'

'Things aren't as bad as they used to be.'

He remembered the May Day parades when they had all had to march through the streets celebrating their sub-servience. And the lectures; the agitation centres where you played at being a devout critic of the infallible; the spontaneous testimonials issued at calculated intervals to district organisers, Party chiefs, the President, the time-servers . . .

'Solidarity,' muttered Ladislav as though he had just thought up a new dirty word.

A man in stained brown overalls lowered himself on to a creaking chair at the next table. With his elbows propped on the table he seemed to stare at them.

They talked about the plans for a new underground tramway system in Prague, but gave up when they found that neither of them was really interested. Ladislav said something about some unidentifiable shards and a fragment of mosaic found during the blasting of foundations for the new Parliament building. Jan said: 'I bet our old friend Brok . . . ' And at the same moment Ladislav said: 'What theories will have to be twisted to fit?' They both laughed, realising they were talking shop. It had always been tacitly agreed that they would not do this when they met in the evenings. They decided to go home.

Jan found Blanka in the sitting-room watching a television programme which he knew she disliked. It was called *Answer Ten Times* — a cumulative quiz series in which contestants tried to stay a more and more gruelling course. If he switched it on unthinkingly at any time, Blanka would say, 'Oh, that rubbish,' and march across the room to switch it off. But now when he came into the room she hastily dropped a magazine whose pages she had been turning and stared fixedly at the screen.

'Hello,' he said.

She scowled to indicate that she could not bear to be interrupted.

Jan sat down to watch the remainder of

the programme. A question floated into his consciousness, and abstractedly he said: 'Tycho Brahe ... no, Keppler, after he had been Brahe's assistant.' When Blanka realised that he was following it, she got up and switched off and said: 'Of all the pretentious rubbish ... '

Her cheeks were flushed. Her soft stubby fingers locked together. He waited. She said: 'Well?'

'Well?'

'Your precious Adamec.'

'He didn't sign.'

She sat down again and let her hands fall limply into her lap. Still he waited. She wouldn't give in this easily.

In a friendly way, as though they were in the habit of discussing all their plans amiably every evening, Blanka said: 'When's your next trip to England?'

He had already given her the full timetable. But he said levelly: 'The November conference in Cambridge.'

'When are you going to take me with you?'

'Blanka, you know we can't both be out

of the country together.'

'I know,' she said plaintively but without raising her voice, 'that you don't even bother to ask.'

'They wouldn't consider it.'

'You enjoy yourself, don't you? You don't want me there to spoil it.'

It was a campaign they had fought before. She was still in an impregnable position. She derided his affection for England but complained because she would not be allowed to go with him and see it for herself. If she had been able to accompany him, she would have determined in advance not to enjoy the trip. But because it was ordained that she must in any case stay at home as a hostage against his possible defection, she could grumble at will about the unfairness of it.

He said: 'I shall be tied up the whole time. Even if you could come, you'd be on your own. You know how . . . ' He restrained himself from predicting how peevish she would be if left to her own devices. 'You'd feel lost,' he said.

'How do you think I feel now?'

44

She was small, almost stocky, but her legs were slim and she had finely boned ankles. When she sat still, not taut or aggressive, she was good to look at. Her breasts were rich, her lips full and soft when they were not tightened in antagonism. If she could only let herself be at ease, let herself be what she had once implicitly promised to be . . .

Jan had not wanted to marry a co-worker in his own field. There had been a shy, nervy, brilliant girl in the Institute, devoted to her work, who would apparently have suited him very well. But it would have been too pat, too uninspiring. They would share interests, be mutually considerate, have a couple of children maybe, and live a neatly balanced private life. In those days it was the tidy, comfortable thing to do. Work and family life — in the bad days there wasn't much else. You looked neither to one side nor to the other; talked to nobody; just did your job, hoped no one would dream up a fantasy in which you could be condemned of deviationism or any of the other new sins, and got what pleasure you could out of your home life.

He resolved to keep the two separate. When so much depended on that enclosed private world, it had to be different from outside occupations. He chose Blanka because she was attractive, impulsive and warming. He laughed at her and with her. She had been brought up as a Catholic but even as a child had decided that priests could not deal with problems the way she wanted them dealt with: instinctively she knew better than they did. During a big recruiting drive she had tried to join the Party, whose persecution of the Church surely put it on the side of the angels; but proved so argumentative that it was unwilling to accept her. Which proved that the Party, too, was wrong.

Impetuously she walked out of a job in a costume jewellery factory and talked herself into an office in Radio Prague two days before she married Jan. They both laughed and agreed they couldn't fail to be happy together. He needed her, she needed him. They would be different, clashing, complementary.

It took him time to learn that impetuosity could be enervating when you were shut up with it in a confined space.

He blamed himself for being unable to match her shifting moods — her passions, tantrums, despairs and attempted ecstasies. Blanka blamed him, too. The harder he tried, the more she blamed him.

At first he had been anxious to show her off to friends and colleagues. He invited them home and enjoyed the envy of the other men. But Blanka's unheralded, fitful storms became an embarrassment; he couldn't calm them and couldn't make a joke of them. She was capable of becoming savagely drunk within thirty minutes, slurring her sneers and abuse until everyone had gone uncomfortably home, and then of sobering up into immediate contempt.

He ceased to ask people in. It was just as well, anyway. Mutual entertaining aroused suspicions: by Party logic, any grouping of two or more families must be an incipient counter-revolutionary cell. So you retreated into your own burrow, into a closeness of family love or hatred.

And hatred led nowhere.

The most dangerous thing he could do was to ask Blanka after one of her bouts, first lovingly and then, in time, despairingly: 'Why . . . ?'

But one of Blanka's first principles was that she owed nobody an explanation of anything she did or thought. It was the others who must justify themselves.

Now, again, she said: 'Well? How do you think I feel? Do you know what it's like for me, here, while you go off abroad, enjoying yourself?'

'Things are getting so much easier,' he said. 'Don't let's rush it. Perhaps next time — '

'Next time? What makes you think there'll be a next time? You think you can go on flourishing your petty defiance at Brok and still be allowed out? They'll clamp down. *I* would, in their shoes. All the things we could do . . . what we could have . . . if you didn't insist on making difficulties.'

She wanted him to stick his neck out and ask to take her abroad with him. At the same time she blamed him for not playing along with the Broks, not conforming.

'You'll have to leave it to me,' he said patiently. 'You'll just have to trust me.'

'Trust you? When I don't know from one day to the next what new stupidity you'll be up to?' Vengefully, with unrestrained glee, she shouted: 'But I'm sure of one thing. They'll soon be stopping your little jaunts.'

★ ★ ★

The threat was absurd. He put it out of his mind. But an echo came jangling discordantly back only two days later when he was called to the telephone at the Institute.

'Professor Melisek? Professor Jan Melisek?'

'Speaking.'

'My name's Veselka. Of the Passport and Visa Office.'

'Nothing wrong, is there?'

'Nothing wrong at all. Nothing to worry about. Just a formality. But I would like to have a talk with you.'

Jan felt very cold. Blanka's jeering prediction throbbed louder than before in his head. 'Where's your office?' he asked as steadily as he could manage. 'I can drop in whenever it suits you.'

Did one have to be so obsequious? Yes, one did.

'I'd prefer to come and see you at your flat, if you don't mind.'

'This evening?'

'Late afternoon would suit me better. If you can get away at such short notice, that is.'

'Yes. Yes, I can get away.'

'Your wife will be at home?'

'Not until later.'

'Good. Then we can talk freely.'

Freely. About what?

Veselka turned out to be a thin man with heavy-lidded eyes. He might have been a year or two younger than Jan. His left cheek was mottled by a sandpapering of pock-marks. When he took his hat off it was to reveal a cul-de-sac of baldness driven up into his lank hair, as though a barber had freakishly designed a pathway with his razor.

Jan had laid a small clip of documents on the table: copies of his visa applications were fastened to letters of invitation from British archaeological societies, the Cambridge conference organisers and his English publisher.

He pushed them towards Veselka, who waved them dismissively away.

'I am not really from the Passport and Visa Office, Professor. I am from . . . somewhere else. I think you can help us. I very much hope you can.'

3

Of course he was not wearing a uniform. Some of them liked to pace about town in pseudo-military raincoats with their hats pulled forward at an angle. But the better ones must, logically, look nondescript.

Jan said bluntly: 'S.T.B.?'

Veselka looked pained. He was not used to being asked questions as direct as this.

'All I want,' he said, 'is a little help.'

'What sort of help?'

Veselka smiled. It was meant to be a worldly-wise smile, an appeal from one intelligent man to another.

'Let's just relax. And talk.'

His gaze lingered on a glass which had been left on the bookcase. Jan took the hint. 'You'd care for a drink? I've got beer. And a little slivovice.'

'You wouldn't have a drop of whisky?'

Jan opened the cupboard. There was a third of a bottle left, conserved since his last trip to London. He was in the habit of drinking it sparingly.

Veselka nodded. 'From England.'

'Scotland, actually,' said Jan with self-conscious pedantry.

'You understand the nuances of these matters.'

They sat on opposite sides of the table. Jan drank, and wondered why the taste of the whisky should be so wrong in this company. He waited for the inquisition or whatever it was to begin.

At last Veselka said 'You are often in England.'

'Not all that often.'

'You have more opportunities than most of us.'

'It's all part of my work.'

'Naturally. A conference, a symposium — London last year, Cambridge this. And you must visit your publisher. Are you preparing another book for foreign translation?'

'You seem to know a lot about me,' said Jan: 'how is it you don't know *that* — or do you?'

Veselka seemed pleased rather than

offended by this challenge. Swilling whisky round the back of his teeth and swallowing, he said: 'You have many connections in England. Even a few relatives, I believe.'

'My mother's sister, and a second cousin. We have nothing in common.'

It was true, yet he felt an obscure guilt, as though by saying it he was somehow betraying someone — not someone he cared for, yet someone who ought not even to be spoken of to a man like this.

'But you do see them sometimes.'

'My aunt feels slighted if I don't make the effort to have tea with her just once when I'm over.'

'And the cousin?'

Veselka's glass was empty. Jan was not going to refill it right away. Let the bastard wait.

'I think you know all about him, too,' he said.

Veselka stared into his empty glass. Jan finished his own drink. Then, angry with himself, he reached for the bottle and poured more whisky for both of them. Curtly he said:

'My cousin has a job in the Ministry of Defence. I fancy he regards me as a bit of an embarrassment. Somewhere in a file it must be recorded that he has a relative who lives in a Communist country — so he's not entirely a good risk.'

'How foolish of them.'

'It's the same everywhere, I imagine.'

'Is it?'

'Isn't it?'

Veselka said: 'Professor Melisek, the world is in a very disturbed condition.'

'So I've noticed.'

'We and our allies have sought for years now to establish a peaceful balance in Europe. Even faced by the revanchist policies of Bonn we have refused to be stampeded into violent measures. Patiently we have tried to attain a detente for the good of all mankind. Britain, of which you are personally so fond, not merely betrayed our country in 1938 but has since shown itself hostile to all the formative elements in our socialist reconstruction these last twenty years. Yet still we and our allies, especially our brothers of the Soviet Union, seek an honourable co-existence. I am sure you, a worker of the mind, will agree . . . '

Jan was finding it hard to listen. His attention wandered, as it had so often done during those interminable political lectures which had droned on throughout the Stalinist years. Jargon had fogged the intellect. Sentences had been shuffled and reshuffled like a child's building blocks — 'It *is* a great big beautiful castle, I tell you it *is*, it's *not* a rotten old rubbish tip' — to mean what you wanted them to mean; or, rather, to mean what certain people wanted them to mean.

The 'free discussion' groups they had been forced to arrange in the Institute; the diktats they were obliged to read in order to know what line to take in their own specialised work; the efforts of some of his colleagues to find Marxist-Leninist interpretations of Salzmunde and Ohrozim culture ('a true worker-peasant manifestation debased by the eventual invasions of the Teutones, carrying the seeds of personality-cult feudalism and exploitation') . . . he had gone through it all before and had learned to dissociate his conscious mind from it.

Here came all the old jargon again, spilling out of Veselka's mouth. But more insidious, supposedly more man-to-man, even with a humorous flicker that hinted one didn't have to take every word as gospel — you and I know better, don't we? — but that for practical purposes it was a good thing to adopt some standards.

'We still have enemies in the West,' Veselka was saying. 'We wish to co-operate, but we must be vigilant. And that is where you can help us. You know many people in England. With your contacts — '

'Now, wait a minute — '

'You are known there, and respected.' Veselka bobbed his head with a half-mocking deference suggesting that this, too, was a bit of a joke. 'You can help your country without harming anyone else.'

'Playing at spies isn't my forte.'

'Spies, Professor? Please let us not be crude. It's only a matter of . . . information.'

'What's the distinction? And what kind of information, anyway? Reports on new

building round Stonehenge and Ave-
bury?'

Veselka's smile stayed fixed, confirming
the good-humoured bond between them.
He said:

'Since you mention buildings . . . well,
there might be a house in London — in
some suburb, say — which on the surface
is a normal, respectable small business,
but in fact is something else. Underneath
there's other activity going on. We'd want
a report on it.'

'I'd be hopeless at that kind of thing.'

'You are an observant man. Trained to
assess probabilities from surface evidence.
What is a lot of your work, Professor, if
not a series of inspired guesses from
observable facts?'

'I'm not playing,' said Jan firmly.

Veselka's expression grew wistful. 'I
want you to think it over.'

'No.'

'Do let me make it clear that we
wouldn't want you to involve your friends
in any distress. Far from it. But tactfully
you could learn a lot from them — and
from the country you know so well.'

'I've told you, I'd be hopeless.'

'If you would just help us when we ask,' said Veselka. 'That's all.'

He turned the glass between his fingers. Now there would be a threat. There must be a screw, and Veselka must now begin to turn it.

Veselka said: 'If . . . '

Then a key clicked in the outer door. Blanka crossed the hall and came through the kitchen into the sitting-room. Her face was flushed from the climb up the three steep flights of stone stairs. She dumped her shopping bag on the floor. 'You should have told me. If we have a visitor, you should have telephoned.'

'Mr Veselka,' said Jan. 'My wife.'

Veselka stood up and held out his hand. 'It is entirely my fault, Mrs Meliskova. I got in touch with your husband at very short notice.'

Grudgingly she took off her glove to shake hands with him. Jan sensed her gradual thaw: Veselka was staring intently at her, and she liked to be concentrated on. She went on with an air of annoyance, jerkily unbuttoning her coat, but imperceptibly she changed. When her coat was off she did not toss it aside but draped it over the back of a chair and moved gracefully across the room.

Veselka watched every movement.

Blanka patted her hair. She looked at Jan and then full at Veselka again. Her wide eyes had in them a myopic intensity which sometimes seemed to indicate astonishment, sometimes greed. It made her appear gratifyingly awestruck when she was listening to someone — preferably a man.

Veselka said: 'I think I have taken up enough of your time, Professor.'

'You mustn't leave just because I'm here,' Blanka pouted.

'No.' He looked at her legs. 'No, I assure you.'

Jan saw Veselka to the door.

'Don't give me your answer now,' said Veselka. 'I'll call you again. Think about it.'

Jan closed the door and went back into the flat. Blanka had taken the armchair by the bookcase and was stretching and yawning, making a show of being sultry and indolent. 'I'm like a cat,' she had once said complacently. 'A domestic cat, that's all I want to be. All you have to do is stroke me, and I'll purr.' She never admitted that she was equally liable to scratch.

Now she said: 'Who was that? We haven't seen him before, have we?'

'He was from . . . ' Jan hesitated. He hadn't had time to make up his mind about how he would deal with Veselka and what he ought to tell Blanka. He said: 'From the Passport and Visa office.'

'There's something wrong?'

He tried to persuade himself that he was exaggerating the spontaneous malice in her face.

'Nothing,' he said. 'A couple of technicalities.'

'And did you ask him?'

'Ask him what?'

'About me,' cried Blanka. 'You had him here — did you ask him whether I could come with you? This time, next time . . . any time?'

He thought of her with him in London

or Cambridge, and was appalled by his own instinctive recoil.

'It wasn't that sort of conversation,' he said. 'It's not his job, that part of it.'

'Did you *ask?*'

'No.'

'You don't want me to come with you.'

'You know it's a waste of time talking about it. You know how their minds work. Someone has to be left behind. If we'd had children, we might both have been let out provided they stayed behind while we were away.'

'You're blaming me again,' she said, 'because we haven't got any children.'

'I've never blamed you. You know that.'

'All I know is that you don't want me to come with you.' She groped for a new barb and found it. 'A hostage,' she said scornfully: 'you think they're naïve enough to suppose you wouldn't defect if it suited you? They're stupid enough to think you care ten hellers for what happens to me?'

'I don't know what they think or why they think it. I just know the way things work out in practice.'

'Mr Jasik's always taking his wife on trips with him.'

'To Bulgaria.'

'That's something, anyway.'

'I'll take you to Bulgaria next spring, if you like.'

'I don't want to go to Bulgaria. I want to go and see this wonderful England of yours.'

'Oh, for goodness' sake . . . Talk to that man who was here, then. Veselka. Ask *him*,' snapped Jan. 'He seems able to pull strings, that one.'

'That's what I mean. Why didn't you ask him while you had a chance? Now we may never see him again.'

'Oh, we'll see him again.' Jan reached for the whisky bottle. There wasn't much left. 'He'll be back. I'm pretty sure of that.'

★   ★   ★

In fact in his next call Veselka did not suggest coming to the flat. He proposed a kavarna near the Tyn church. He was slipping off his coat as Jan arrived, and

63

paused to shake hands effusively.

'Coffee, Professor?'

Jan wanted to accept no favours from the man; but if they had to spend time together, he needed something to occupy him.

'A Mattoni, please.'

The mineral water tingled with a sulphurous chill against his tongue. He waited for the next round to begin.

Veselka said affably: 'Western women are promiscuous by nature, I think?'

'What?' Jan was taken aback.

'The women. In England. They are very ready to make advances.'

'Not that I've noticed.'

'You are not interested in women?'

'Not indiscriminately.'

'They enjoy immorality, I have been told. You've never been tempted, while in England . . . ?'

'No.'

'But then, you are happily married.' Veselka broke a piece of sugar and dropped half into his coffee. 'Your wife is charming.'

Jan said: 'You wanted to talk to me.'

'The advertising in magazines,' Veselka went on: 'Western magazines, full of nudes and semi-nudes, titillating the passions, implying that sexual perversions are all that make life tolerable. Erotic propaganda, erotic books . . . ' He gulped at his coffee and appeared to burn his mouth, for he had to wipe it hastily with the back of his hand. 'We have been shown American films . . . '

'Degrading,' said Jan ironically.

Veselka watched a girl settling herself at a table in the window. She wore black boots with a swaying leather fringe along the tops, and a short skirt. She put a hand inside her blouse to adjust a shoulder strap.

'I can't stay long,' said Jan.

Veselka started up what showed signs of becoming another lecture on Western perfidy, then seemed to lose interest. He ordered another coffee and a mineral water. At a tangent he asked a few questions about Jan's work on excavations in North Bohemia, but they were random questions and he hardly listened to the replies.

Abruptly he said: 'You know Mr Gregg?'

'Gregg?' It came so unexpectedly that Jan was puzzled for a moment.

Veselka grinned as though he had succeeded in springing a neat little trap. 'You don't deny you know Mr Gregg at the Embassy?'

'Oh, the British Embassy. Of course I know him.'

'You're very good friends, I think.'

'He has been very helpful. He arranges conferences here, and he's made many introductions for me in England.'

'He has never asked you for any special information?'

Jan sat very still for a few seconds, then said: 'Special, or specialised?'

'You're playing with words.'

'No,' said Jan. 'I value them too much.'

'He has never tried to enlist you in any activities on behalf of the West?'

'That's not his kind of job, any more than it's mine.'

'Oh, Professor.' Veselka shook his head. The gesture was as false and badly timed as the movements of an amateur actor.

'You are so very naïve, Professor Melisek. Men in such positions are there because of certain abilities. Let us be frank: their nominal jobs are rarely the true ones.'

'Just because our people in London are specially planted, there's no reason to suppose everybody else . . . '

Jan stopped. This was going too far.

Veselka said smoothly: 'You've noticed failings in our attachés in London? Their methods are too obvious — too crude?'

'I know nothing at all about their methods.'

'They could do our cause great damage if they go about things clumsily. Do tell me — '

'I know nothing about them. I've been to a couple of receptions at the Embassy, that's all.'

'As a detached observer, your views could be most valuable. Between friends, Professor . . . '

Jan stood up. 'I must go.'

Veselka looked mildly surprised. 'I was hoping we would have a lot to say to each other. A lot more.'

'I'm afraid not.'

'Perhaps next time.'

Jan walked briskly for five minutes, then slowed and tried not to let the knot of impotent fury tighten too agonisingly inside himself. He was not going to see Veselka again. He would do nothing for him: nothing. He had done no wrong, there was no reason to fear; he wasn't some wretched puppet to be jerked this way and that by contemptible bully-boys.

He walked down to the embankment. There was no wind. The surface of the Vltava was like slowly drifting oil, reflecting the quivering spires and smudges of pastel colour.

Prague was a soft city, a gentle city: no clear, harsh edges and no strident architecture; a graceful, nostalgic, crumbling place.

And under its heavy arcades, in offices behind ponderous walls, in rooms overlooking dark inner courtyards, a thousand grubby little functionaries like Veselka worked assiduously away, contaminating everything they touched.

He crossed the river and walked home.

Blanka had quarrelled with a young producer in the Radio. Things were easier when she was in this mood. Her tendency to over-dramatise everything became, in such instances, entertaining; and when she knew that Jan was really listening and enjoying the performance, she played up to him and they both laughed.

Even so, there was an underlying bitterness which could too easily come to the surface.

She resented being confined to Programme Allocations Section. She had wanted to be on the production side — had asked for transfers, sure she could do the job better than most of the pretentious young men and fading hacks she had to deal with. The keeping of records and marking up of schedules was unworthy of her. The job brought her in contact with a wide range of people, and at first she had enjoyed the variety; but now she was soured by the conviction that she was wasted in non-creative tasks while her inferiors blundered on into more rewarding positions.

Jan listened, sympathised and made a joke. They ate, and drank half a bottle of Ludmila. When he said he must shut himself away in the other room and do an hour's work, Blanka smiled as though it didn't matter at all.

But he knew that when he approached the door she would speak. She could not bear to let him go out of a room without reaching out verbally to delay him. Often what she said made no sense: it was simply that she had to see how long she could keep him teetering there. If he cut her off in mid-sentence or slid away before she was ready to let go, it only proved that she was justified in believing that he neglected her.

'Jan.' Here it came. 'Have you seen that man again — the one who was here the other evening?'

'No reason why I should see him again,' he said cautiously.

'I just wondered.'

There was something odd in her appraising smile. She was confident that she had scored off him in some way.

'It's all settled,' he said.

'Is it?'

'It was just a formality. I told you — a couple of technicalities.'

'Yes,' she said, 'that's what you told me.'

Incongruously her expression reminded him of Veselka's.

He went on into the other room before she could goad him into whatever skirmish she might have in mind.

The hour's work he had promised himself did not materialise. He leafed through half a dozen books in succession and tried to make coherent notes. He might just as well have been skimming through a travel brochure.

Blanka moved about in the kitchen. She was humming to herself. Normally it wouldn't have disturbed him — he would have been glad that she was in a good mood — but this evening he made it an excuse for his own inability to concentrate, and knew it was an excuse and a poor one at that.

He was frightened.

It was all very well to get up and walk

out on Veselka. A fine assertion of one's right to pick and choose one's own company and one's own timetable.

But there would be another telephone call.

He would refuse to go; or refuse to have the man in the flat.

But might it not be better to play along?

Think. An intelligent man ought surely to be capable of beating such a creature at his own shoddy game. Think. Anticipate the next approach, be ready for the threats that would surely be intensified. Keep him guessing for a week or two while you say you're making up your mind. Play the absent-minded professor so that he gives up in disgust. Or accept one mission, get to England, and make such a mess of it that they never ask again. Bring back a pack of lies. Be cunning or obtuse: which was better?

It would soon be time to apply for his visa for the Cambridge trip.

For years the barriers had been down. Then, as Stalin's monstrous statue on Letna crashed into ruin, they were raised.

Could he bear them to descend again, shutting him in?

He spent next day cataloguing bronze armlets and brooches for an exhibition which was to be mounted in the Hradcany vaults. It was straightforward work but he found that he had made three slipshod mistakes. From then on he checked and rechecked every item, and finished the day with a headache.

Blanka was home first. She was waiting to greet him with a deceptively casual taunt: 'I hear Mr Jasik is to have a chalet in the rest centre outside Konopiste. It's beautiful down there.'

'We could have taken over that summerhouse from the Smutny, but you didn't want it.'

'You get this one maintained free.'

His head throbbed. He kissed her, and went to his chair in the sitting-room, leaving the door open to make it clear that he was not shutting her out.

Blanka followed him in.

'You'd sooner smash things than accept them and make the best of them, wouldn't you?' she said.

73

It was an odd thing for her to say. Jan thought of the painstaking hours and days he had spent, stooped over tiny fragments of pottery, constructing historical jigsaw puzzles. And he sensed that once more the words she used meant nothing in themselves. She was seething with some strange wildness, that could turn just as readily to hysterical gaiety as to fury.

'It's always the same,' she burst out. 'That time you crossed the flats representative downstairs — '

'He was hounding that woman on the first floor.'

'Her husband was in prison.'

'On a trumped-up charge.'

'You could have had us both thrown in with him, the way you talked.'

She blundered deliberately into the table so that she would have an excuse for cursing it, then let herself slide down to the floor with her back to the divan. 'What's the use?' She put her hands on the floor and let her head sag back. 'What's the use?'

End of scene, thought Jan. Quite a short one. Blanka would get up in a minute and prepare supper.

He let himself sink back into his chair.

Blanka's eyes were shut. He studied her drawn face and tried to think himself into believing that somehow they could still be happy. Her throat was still smooth, her high colour still made her look like a bright, sparkling country girl. The pose was one of long-suffering agony, but could equally well have been an invitation — her breasts taut, her head back, her hands braced against the floor.

Abruptly she opened her eyes and met his gaze. She let out a little sigh, then brought her head forward in drooping submission.

'You used to like me to sit on the floor,' she said.

From tetchiness to plaintive reproach, then on to sly invitation. The irritation and the mawkishness were all essential ingredients of her orgasm.

'I don't know why you put up with me,' she said.

She edged across the floor, her head falling even farther forward so that her hair tumbled over her face.

Jan said, defensively flippant: 'It hasn't been such an ordeal.' He surprised himself by a sudden snarl to match her own: 'I've never wanted anyone else.'

'Perhaps you ought to have done. Perhaps . . . Jan, perhaps you ought to beat me.' Her voice thickened. 'That's what I deserve. You know, if you'd been tougher with me from the start, I'd have been a better wife to you.'

Her head lay against his knee. Looking down at the creamy nape of her neck he saw that while moving across the floor she had contrived to unfasten two of the cloth-covered buttons.

Contrived. Yes, that was the word.

He shut out the drably analytical thought. All it really meant was that she wanted him.

He put his hand over the opening between the buttons. Her flesh was warm. She flinched as he touched her, then pushed herself gently upwards against his fingertips. It was enough. He wanted her.

She moaned as they went down together on the carpet. He fought to hold her steady while she abandoned herself to sobbing convulsions. His thumbs bit into her. She gritted her teeth and arched up as though in a despairing attempt to unsaddle him.

At last, satiated, she went limp.

There was a draught under the door.

She was waiting for him to get up. She liked him to make the first move: liked to feel he wanted to leave her before she was ready for him to go.

When he slid away, she sighed and sat up. There were two red marks where his thumbs had gripped her. Blanka touched one of them. 'They'll be blue by tomorrow,' she said huskily. 'You once promised to keep renewing them, so they'd never wear out. But you don't love me.'

'What more do you want?' He tried to keep it light although he knew the attempt was doomed.

'You have to *try*, don't you? You have to make an effort to love me — to make love to me. You're all right once you're started, but you don't actually *want* me all the time, do you? You have to think yourself into the right mood. Have to *think*.'

And if he didn't make the effort, he would be just as much to blame. Either way, she would complain.

They gathered up their clothes. The room looked bleak now. Inside she probably felt as cold and forlorn as he did.

She said: 'If you loved me . . . '

'Blanka.' He spoke so sharply that she jumped, and looked at him half hopefully. 'Don't spoil it,' he said. 'That was good. Don't pretend it wasn't.'

'It was good,' she admitted. 'Jan . . . if it was like that all the time . . . I mean, if it was like that and you really meant it . . . But if you really meant it, everything else would be easier as well.'

'Everything else?'

'Everything,' she shouted. The mood splintered. The jagged edges were there again. 'But you don't want things to be easy, do you? You won't sign this, won't listen to that, won't be polite to Mr Veselka when he could do so much for us.'

He pushed his head through his shirt. 'Who says so?'

'You just won't be sensible.'

'What do you know about Veselka?'

'Don't shout at me. I'm your wife, you owe me something. I work hard for both of us, without stirring up trouble — why can't *you*? I don't see why I should — '

'Blanka,' he said, 'has Veselka been to see you?'

'It's all part of his job. Purely routine.'

'What did he say?'

'He was nice enough. Very sweet, in fact.'

'Look, you know he's State Security, don't you? You do realise that? S.T.B.'

'He might be.'

'You know he is. You can smell them a mile away.'

'That's just the sort of thing you'd say — just the sort of thing to get us into trouble sooner or later.'

'What did you tell him?'

'I've got nothing to be ashamed of.'

'Nobody's saying you have. But what did he get out of you?'

'He didn't get anything out of me.' She threw her clothes on to the divan and picked them up one by one, wriggling

79

into them. 'He's rather impressive, really. He's a real live person.'

'Do you know what they're like, that lot? Do you know the nice little methods they have?'

'I know it's better to be reasonable with them,' she retorted. 'Jan, to make things easier for both of us, couldn't you . . . couldn't you . . . ?'

* * *

The next day there was another telephone call to the Institute. Veselka suggested a meeting in a little place off Wenceslas Square. Nothing special. Just a chat.

A crowd was forming up at the traffic lights on Wenceslas Square as Jan approached. He felt hopelessly isolated. He felt a wild desire to lash out and grab someone, the first man who came to hand, and be arrested and hustled off. If he was going to be persecuted, at least let it be for something concrete, something ordinary and identifiable. But there was no reason to grab anyone; no point in making a scene.

He wondered if he had been followed from the Institute. But that would be futile, since Veselka had an appointment with him and they would know where he was.

They . . .

He wondered if they would follow him when he left Veselka. Whether, perhaps, he was always followed now.

But why?

Most of all he wondered why. The silent shout screeched through his mind: Why pick on *me*?

4

It was too ordinary a place for secret discussions. Or for threats.

A woman who had been spending vouchers at Tuzex came in laden with corn flakes, tomato ketchup and Dutch chocolate. Two earnest young men at the next table argued about a film which neither of them had seen but about which they had strong opinions. An elderly man sat with a half-empty glass of mineral water and read a newspaper on a stick.

Jan had intended to challenge Veselka outright about his visit — or had there been more than one? — to Blanka. But without any preamble Veselka, more affable than ever, started discussing holidays. Some folk liked the Tatras. Magnificent landscapes, of course. For himself, he had been brought up in the country but had always found it dull. There was nowhere in the world like Prague.

'Nowhere?' said Jan. 'You've travelled a lot?'

It was a stupid provocation. Veselka's left eyelid dipped slightly, and that was all. He went on to talk about train travel, planes and cars.

'You have a Skoda, I think?'

'Brilliant deduction.' Without a great deal of foreign currency, there wasn't much else you could have.

'The trouble is maintaining them. Our roads shake you to pieces, eh? We have a lot to learn.'

A lot to learn — from other countries? He wondered if Veselka was tempting him to say this.

'You'll soon be off on one of your trips,' Veselka went on.

'A couple of weeks from now.'

'But you fly, of course. You don't take your car.'

The discussion was meaningless. Perhaps the idea was to numb you with platitudes, until incautiously you said something which could be recorded against you.

Veselka said: 'I hope you're allowing

yourself some free time in England, to play the tourist?'

'I've got a tight programme.'

'You work too hard, my dear fellow. You know, if you wished to extend your stay there would be no official objections at this end. Take another day — do some sightseeing.'

'I've seen Cambridge before.'

'Have you ever been to Suffolk?'

Jan thought back. 'Once. I was driven for an afternoon to Bury St Edmunds. A wonderful afternoon.'

'You should go farther than that. Out to the coast.'

'You know it?' said Jan sceptically.

Above Veselka's left eyebrow was a narrow but deep furrow, like an old scar when he frowned. He said: 'We have our information.'

'Good. Then you won't be relying on me for any.'

Veselka leaned across the table. 'Professor, I thought we were becoming friends. I thought we understood one another.'

'I think we do. Very well indeed.'

'So.'

Out of contempt rather than comradeship, Jan signalled the waiter and ordered two more beers. Veselka smiled as though this signified complete accord between them, and went on:

'There is a research establishment on the Suffolk coast, on a spit of land off Orford. One of the easternmost tips of the British Isles . . . devoted, Professor, to the development of secret weapons, eventually supplied to British and American air squadrons in Norfolk and Suffolk, all waiting for an excuse to take off and destroy everything we believe in. Purely offensive . . . destructive.'

Don't know that I blame them, thought Jan. Aloud he said: 'Right outside my field.' Drily he added: 'I've never even handled a gun. I did my military service down the mines.'

'Yes.' Veselka didn't need telling this. 'And I'm sure you don't approve of horror weapons — civilian murder, indiscriminate killing.'

'I think one should discriminate,' Jan agreed gently.

'And your English friends? Would they

approve, if they really knew what was going on? I don't think so. Professor, I wouldn't dream of asking you to do anything against your real friends. To be quite honest' — he smiled his gratitude for the beer he was drinking — 'none of this is *my* line, really. But one of my colleagues is interested.'

'I shall be fully occupied in Cambridge.'

'There are two houses in Orford. We could be interested in them.'

'If you're genuinely interested,' said Jan, 'in England they have men called estate agents.'

'One of the houses is for sale. It over-looks the river, set back half a kilometre. There is another in the village itself.'

'If you know this much, you must already have somebody on the spot.'

'We like to have confirmation.'

'You don't trust a soul, do you? Check and double-check.'

'It saves errors, in the end.'

Jan said: '*Quis custodiet . . .* '

Veselka stared blankly. 'You have your diary with you?'

'I'm not making any dates for house-hunting. When I get to England I'll be so busy — '

'If you get to England.'

Veselka said it as quietly as though it were a joke they had often shared before, so that there was no need to do more than quote the tag-line.

'If you mean — '

'All I mean,' said Veselka, 'is that I'd like you to have the addresses. If you have time to go there, all well and good. If not . . . we shall understand.'

Jan tingled with an anticipation of loss, like a child told there will be no summer holiday, no special treat, nothing ever again.

But he did not take out his diary.

'I can't promise anything,' he said stiffly.

'Of course not. All we want is what help you can offer. Just to tell us what the view from the house is — perhaps inquire about the man selling, ask if you can see over it . . . Leave us to evaluate what you bring us.'

And evaluate me, thought Jan. A trial, a dummy run. Sentence postponed.

Veselka took out a slip of paper and wrote two addresses on it. He pushed the paper across the table. Jan sat and looked at it. He could tear it up here and now and drop the shreds in the ashtray. Or he could pick it up and put off making a decision — or, rather, put off declaring that decision.

He picked it up. It was cowardly. But it meant he would have one more trip to England. Just one.

As he folded the paper and tucked it into his wallet, he said with sullen defiance, ameliorating his surrender: 'Without a car . . . '

'I leave it to you. I am sure you will manage.'

And if he did — if he showed himself a good, obedient boy? Veselka's approval, Blanka's approval. Everything easier all round.

Veselka sat back. Business was finished. They could enjoy each other's company. 'Cars,' he said with a knowing shrug. 'I suppose you have the same trouble as I do. Maintenance. It's getting worse. You know, we'll soon be back in a society where barter is the only way of doing business. Money's no use.'

Jan was almost certain he knew what was coming.

'You get your car repaired,' said Veselka airily, 'only if you've got something to offer in exchange. He repairs your car, you do a few Sunday afternoons digging foundations for his summerhouse. No money changes hands. It's the only way nowadays.'

There was nothing illegal in such arrangements, yet Veselka's manner implied there was something seedy about them, not quite worthy of a distinguished savant.

And how had he found out, anyway?

Jan said: 'I believe you've approached my wife.'

'Ah. Mrs Meliskova. Charming. You're a lucky fellow, Professor.'

'I'd prefer you to deal with me and not with my wife. She doesn't understand the situation.'

'I had the impression she understood it very well.'

Jan looked at his watch. Veselka flicked his fingers at the waiter. 'Together?' asked the waiter. 'No,' said Jan quickly; then, driven by an even more violent loathing than before, he said: 'Yes — here.'

'No, no.' Veselka lifted a deprecating hand. But he allowed Jan to pay. When they got up he put his arm briefly round Jan's shoulders. 'Thank you. I do enjoy meeting you, you know.'

At the door he added: 'I hope you have a rewarding time in Cambridge. And do make arrangements to stay that extra day. There'll be no opposition, I promise.'

Jan watched him go. He was pricked by an impulse to follow, to see if Veselka really went back to Perstyn, to follow just for the sake of following and confirm that Veselka was what he claimed to be.

But then, Veselka had never claimed to be anything.

There were things that didn't need to be spoken; things better left, anyway, unspoken.

⋆　⋆　⋆

Jan sat in a restaurant in Cambridge, alone. It was one of his rarest pleasures. He savoured it all — colours, lights, shifting faces, buzz of voices, everything — with an acute physical awareness. He wished the service were not so good: he would have preferred the meal to take a long time, with long gaps between courses. In Prague he could have made it last an entire evening. But then, in Prague there was little incentive to serve the customer quickly: you got the same pay whether you worked well or badly, fast or slow, and the tips were meagre. Here the service was efficient because they wanted the customer to leave and make way for another. The profit motive, of course. And in Prague . . . lack of profit motive? How would Veselka make his theories — or, rather, his catch-phrases — fit that?

Don't think about Veselka. Not here.

He reached for his wine-glass. The stem was cool between his fingers. Here he was, holding a glass; these were his cuffs, this the texture of his jacket. Wine the colour of honey, distorting the shapes and hues of three people on the far side of the restaurant.

The feeling of achievement, of simply

being here at all . . .

Another few hours of his life that he would treasure, look back on . . .

Look back? Already he was hoarding up against the miserly future, when this would be only something to remember. He tried to make himself even more aware of the present, to hold on to it. Why could there never be a *now?*

A blonde in an ice-blue dress passed his table. The waiter and a young man fussed round her chair. She glanced at Jan as she sat down, then allowed herself a cool, longer look.

Of course the scene needed a beautiful woman to complete it. Preferably at his own table, not at that one. The texture of skin, the different music in a woman's voice, the whole new counterpoint of sound and taste and smell.

But that was a different game, the one of pursuit, flattery, mutual deception. There wasn't enough time. And involvement meant the blurring of immediate pleasure, the mixing of flavours into indistinctness.

All too complicated and disruptive. He

had never wanted anyone else but Blanka. Or had never allowed himself to want anyone else but Blanka. She had despised him for it. To her it was a sign of weakness, of sexual dullness. For Blanka, loyalty was not an essential ingredient of love.

Jan raised his glass to the ideal present, not to any person or theory. The blonde glanced at him again, then settled back to let her escort stare deeply into her eyes.

Jan slept soundly that night, and read his paper to the conference next morning with a gusto which, he sensed, some of them found almost vulgar.

Only on the last night in Cambridge did he lie awake, tossing and turning. He had one more day in England and ought to be grateful for it. But the thought of going to Suffolk was beginning to nauseate him. He had pushed the thought itself down all the time he was at the conference or roaming round the city. Now it could be suppressed no longer. Tomorrow he was going to Orford.

It turned out a cold, clear day. He took the train from Cambridge to Ipswich and changed to a two-coach diesel with most of the seats set with their backs to the driver. A sparkling mist clung low to the fields as they bumbled along the line to Woodbridge, then cleared over a bright wideness of water. He had to buy his ticket on the train, rather as though it were a bus. He tucked the scrap of paper into his wallet, along with the ticket to Ipswich, which nobody had collected from him.

There were other tickets and oddments of paper in his various pockets. It was childish to keep such souvenirs, perhaps, but for a few weeks after his return home he would be able to pull a London bus ticket out with his handkerchief, or pretend to be surprised by a crumpled receipt while looking for a postage stamp in his wallet.

At Woodbridge he found a bus for Orford and sat in it for fifteen minutes waiting for it to leave.

He tried to give the scene an added dimension by studying it through someone else's eyes. Suppose Blanka had been in the seat beside him . . .

No. Somehow that distorted everything.

The bus jogged out of the little town and along a winding road through plantations of dark trees. Pines formed up into disciplined avenues. The sky was a frosty blue and somewhere there was pale sunshine, but the woods soaked up no light.

He could almost have been in Bohemia. But he wasn't.

There were five other people on the bus. Two women with shopping baskets, a young man in blue denims, an elderly man wearing a flat checked cap and a man in a dark overcoat who could have been an engineer or a bank manager; or a spy.

He felt sure someone must be watching him.

There was a sign by the roadside, lettered in large red capitals:

CAUTION
SLOW FOR 2 MILES
ORFORD NESS PROJECT

A wonder they didn't put a Russian translation alongside it, just to be helpful!

A street opened out of the trees ahead. There was a scattering of houses, and then a cramped square with the flicker of a castle keep beyond it.

It was quiet.

He walked away from the bus, down the arc of a narrow lane. It gave out on the edge of a shallow creek. He retraced his steps.

When he came upon one of the houses he had been told to investigate, it took him by surprise. It was too real, too solid. It stood some yards from its nearest neighbour, and beyond it was the cold grey-green ridge of the Ness, with a few buildings looking, from this distance, like workmen's huts or Vltava summerhouses.

The house had a 'For Sale' notice pasted over by a diagonal 'Sold' strip.

He could go back and tell Veselka it was off the market. Nothing to be done about it.

But he knew that would not be enough. Veselka would ask questions; then talk about cars, Dukla football team, the price of meat; and ask more questions to find out how assiduous he had been.

He ought to look for the other house. But already his revulsion was so great that he decided to abandon the whole thing here and now. It had been a waste of time coming here: even before seeing the village he had known, really, that he was not going to collaborate.

A sudden group of planes flew over, very low. There was a clamorous obscenity of American jet thunder round the red-tiled roofs. He could imagine what Veselka, or Veselka's skilled prompters, would have to say about that. Dear Professor . . . what is your cherished, idyllic England but an expendable aircraft carrier for Americans, ready to launch their hatred against the East? You could not, after all, get much further East than this in the British Isles.

On the bus, he watched the stark yet drowsy countryside falling away behind him. He was carrying a few fragmentary memories of Orford to add to his uncatalogued store of reminiscences.

Halfway back, he felt a temptation to get off. To sit by the roadside and wait for the next bus back to the village. It might not be for a couple of hours, but no matter. Time here was of no consequence. He would go back and get a job — as what . . . as a fisherman, a road-sweeper, a spy-catcher? — and nobody in Prague would ever know what had happened to him.

They could hardly blame Blanka for his defection. She could sincerely tell them that she had never agreed with any of his views, had hated everything he told her about his trips to England, had always suspected that he would turn traitor in the end. But still she would suffer. That was the whole point. They relied on the conscience of those who were too squeamish to put others at risk. They would pounce on Blanka, even knowing she could have had no part in his flight — not to punish Blanka but to punish him, the defector. Once you knew the rules and knew who would pay the penalties, you couldn't stay out. At the end of your parole you went back.

In Woodbridge he had to wait for a train. The pubs were open and he went into the nearest, more for the sake of listening than drinking. There was no equivalent at home. There, if you went into a café, you might argue politics and religion in an undertone, but it was safer not to. You didn't denounce the authorities and curse the local town council. You didn't go into bars for social drinking. All your real life was at home. And if there was no real life there, then you were very lonely.

From Ipswich he went to London, and had dinner in Soho with his publisher for the last time.

The last time?

He was taking nothing back. His chances of being allowed out again were slim.

For the last time, he resolutely told himself. Every sound and movement must count now. They could not be repeated. Each mouthful was the last.

Anthony Finch was the one remaining member of the family which had founded the publishing house of Finch and Farrell. He was a plump man with curly grey hair and a pink, ingenuous face. His wife was the youngest daughter of an earl, and they had three sons. Jan knew from previous encounters that Finch could not start work in the morning until he had finished *The Times* crossword, that he invariably drank two large pink gins at lunchtime and with religious implacability offered guests a meal built round either a Leoville Barton or a Meursault about which he had some confidential recommendation, and that he had achieved an inexplicitly diplomatic coup in Cyprus before settling into his chair in the family firm.

Finch lived in Surrey and rarely spent a night in town. 'But this is rather a special occasion — one of your rare visits, eh?' It leaked out, as the meal progressed, that he had in fact come to it straight from a cocktail party for another of their authors — a zoologist whose new book on the sexual seasons of the northern hemisphere had already been serialised in a Sunday newspaper, sold paperback rights, and been featured in *Life*. Finch did not state, but allowed it to be inferred, that such books subsidised scholars like Professor Jan Melisek and provided the excellent meal he was eating.

'And the book?' said Finch. 'The big one?'

He was waiting, and had been waiting a long time, for the great popular work on archaeology that Jan Melisek was one day going to produce.

'Not much progress,' Jan confessed.

'Pity. Now's the time, you know. Never been a better market. Archaeology's all the rage, thanks to television. A lively, comprehensive book of the kind I know you could write — really, old chap, it'd make your fortune. And ours, of course.' He chuckled to show that this was the least important factor.

'I don't want to start until I see my way clear,' said Jan. 'At the moment I'm hard pressed. The Institute likes us to work and to be seen working.'

Finch signalled for the sweet trolley to be brought to the table, then recommended the cheese board anyway. When negotiations had been concluded he said:

'How *are* things in your part of the world? Is it true there's a move to pension off old whatsisname?'

'Novotny?'

'That's him. We're dreadfully ignorant over here, you know.' He tasted a sliver of Brie and pursed his lips judicially. 'It's a disgrace that we know so little about what's what, when you think how important it all is.'

Jan said nothing.

'Perhaps,' said Finch with heavy tact, 'you'd sooner not commit yourself.'

'Things are better. The apparatchiks aren't as firmly in control as they used to be. Whether there'll be another swing of the pendulum . . . '

Looking at Finch's cherubic face, glazed into courteous attentiveness, he knew that nothing he said would convey anything to the Englishman. It was all foreign and odd. Characters like Veselka existed in novels published by his firm, but not in his own life.

Jan attacked his cheese and biscuits. Tomorrow he would be on his way home. This year, next year, sometime there might be political changes. A few new attitudes might be struck, there would be manipulations and regroupings; but it would amount to no more than the rearrangement of figures in a waxworks museum. One more variation on the same old drabness . . . How many subtle hues could drabness produce without any fundamental change in itself?

'I don't think I could live under the sort of conditions you have to endure,' said Finch.

'Either you live,' said Jan, 'or you stop living. What else would you suggest?'

Finch looked hurt, as though it were bad taste to take him so literally. He reached for his glass and found only a few drops in the bottom. 'Luigi . . . ' The Italian waiter scurried forward, lifted the bottle in the napkin, and carefully poured wine two-thirds of the way up their glasses. Finch sighed his thankfulness.

Don't think I could live under the sort of conditions . . . What did Finch know about it? You lived because there was no alternative — or not one you could allow yourself to contemplate. You couldn't alter conditions single-handed, and nobody wanted to risk helping you. At any rate Finch had used the right word, just once. Endure. You had to endure. Survive . . . being as honest as possible and at the same time as wary as possible. The two didn't go comfortably together. But what else was there? You couldn't simply and painlessly stop breathing.

Leaving Anthony Finch late that evening, Jan encouraged himself to feel hostile. His last evening, but let there be no dying fall of pleasure. Anger was more sustaining.

These people were impossible. They didn't know and they would never know or want to know. You couldn't communicate with them because in their placid conceit they had long ago ceased to listen.

He was glad to be going home.

But on the Prague-bound TU he felt desolate.

He thought about Blanka.

Things had to be made better between them. He was the one who had to make them better.

What they said to each other had nothing to do with the real situation. They could squabble for hours without ever touching on the things that mattered.

To her his work was dull. He wished she could see it differently, but it wasn't her fault. No reason why he himself should be dull. He wanted to love Blanka as much as she wanted him to love her. He must try, and try not to show he was trying. Try to let it come naturally. An absurd contradiction — making an effort to relax!

At Prague airport it was freezing. Cold air bit at his throat as he crossed from the plane to the main building.

On the far side of the Customs barrier Blanka was waiting for him.

It was an omen. He had been making resolves; she must have been doing the same.

'I thought you'd prefer the car to the airport coach,' she said perkily.

Cold had brightened her cheeks. Her chin was sunk demurely in the bunched-up collar of a lime-green coat.

Jan kissed her. She smelt good. He held her away from him and said: 'That's a new coat.'

'Fancy your noticing. Who'd have thought it?'

The old sharpness was there, strangely tinged with delight. She had sneered to herself that he wouldn't spot it, that it was safe for her to flaunt it; yet she would have been piqued if he had really failed to notice.

Stop analysing . . . stop picking her to pieces!

Why had he thought of her as *flaunting* it?

In Prague itself a dusting of snow bleached the roofs and the hillside gardens on Petrin. The cathedral was a spiky silhouette against the flat grey sky.

The streets were cold. They hurried up the chill stone staircase and into the warmth of their flat.

Blanka took off her new coat and hung it up. He realised that her dress, also, was new, and that she had meant him to realise it. In honour of his home-coming? He would have liked to believe it.

She could have been one of the women he had seen in Cambridge or London. The cut of the brown and green dress was too stylish for Prague: it flamboyantly did not belong here.

He said: 'Where did all this come from?'

'From Tuzex.' She rotated slowly. 'You like it?'

'I knew you could buy bolts of cloth from Tuzex. I didn't know you could get a French dress.'

'Italian. There are lots of things you don't know.'

In any case, she wasn't in the sort of job which entitled her to occasional issues of Tuzex vouchers. Unless a relative overseas had sent foreign currency.

He said: 'You've heard from your cousin?'

'Cousin?' At first she hardly grasped what he meant. Then she said: 'Oh, Jarmila. No. Jarmila knows better than to risk writing to us.'

'Then . . . '

He saw the alarm in her eyes. She was wondering if she had been too blatant. The coat and the dress: what sort of defiance did they represent? She had been so anxious for him to see them, but now her mood switched to one of apprehension and she began to cover up with evasive action. 'Jarmila!' she said too loudly. 'Just think! If it hadn't been for you, I'd probably have left ages ago. I could have escaped with Jarmila when she went, and gone to live with our aunt in Vienna. To *live*!'

'We don't know Jarmila got through. We've never had a word from her.'

'Because she didn't want to make trouble for us.'

'Others have got in touch. It's not that grim, not nowadays. Nobody opens letters.'

'How do you know? And how could *she* be sure, out there? No, Jarmila just didn't want to make trouble. If I'd gone with her — '

'But you didn't want to go, anyway.'

'Sometimes I wonder.'

'You haven't told me about the dress yet,' he said. 'Or the coat.' This wasn't the way he had promised himself he would talk to her when he got home. Somehow it was being forced upon him.

'What do I have to tell you? You can see them for yourself. Of course' — her defensive rage was building up to a scream — 'I don't expect you to like them. I don't expect you to have the taste — '

'How did you get them?'

'I haven't asked you for the money, have I? If I work hard and do my share, it's a pity if I can't buy some new clothes when I feel like it. You've never made a fuss before.'

'It's never been quite this sort of thing before, has it?' He looked at her, waited and repeated softly: 'Has it?'

He was frightened, more than he had been before going away. He didn't know what this new element was, but sensed fearfully that only the slightest provocation was needed for it to be made plain.

★   ★   ★

'So you're married.' Along a straight stretch of road Miss Armitage turned briefly towards him, green-eyed not with jealousy but with grave curiosity. 'Where's your wife now, then?'

Jan shrugged.

'You mean you don't know?'

'I'm not sure.'

He wondered how much he had revealed to her about Blanka and himself. He thought he had given bare facts only, the fewest possible personal touches; but already the conversation of the last twenty minutes belonged to a past as misty as the Iron Age. Was he suffering from delayed shock — quietly delirious, with no control over thoughts, speech or memory?

'You left her behind' — Miss Armitage was incredulous — 'not knowing . . . ?'

'We were separated.'

It sounded non-committal, with no danger of emotion in it. All he could hope was that if he went on talking in English the language itself would alter the proportions of the nightmare: it softened here, clarified there, gave him a new sounding-board; even made him wonder, uneasily, if his actions these last few days made any more sense than his words were making now. Had he panicked too readily?

'You haven't the foggiest idea where she is?'

'No.' Then, his academic puritanism

110

demanding the qualification, he said: 'Not exactly.'

No, he couldn't say precisely where she was. But in general terms . . .

'When you say you were separated, do you mean what we mean in English when . . . ' The girl put her foot down on the accelerator, and after a while, her eyes dispassionately on the road, she said: 'I'm sorry. It's really none of my business.'

He wondered if she regretted having picked him up. Perhaps she was trying to summon up the courage to tell him to get out and walk.

5

Maggie was thirsty. As they drove towards the granite up-thrust of a town, she said:

'Feel like stopping for a drink, or a bite to eat?'

'If you wish.'

She could tell he was not enthusiastic. 'You'd sooner be safely over the frontier?'

'Please, if you want to stop . . . '

'No. Maybe you're right.'

The road curved below the rock on which the town was built, then began to climb, as though pivoting on the slim tower at the peak.

'Where are we?' asked Maggie.

'Tabor.' In an undertone he added wryly: 'Brothers and sisters.'

He spoke as though it were self-explanatory. Did he realise how little of what he had told her made sense? A few intimations of what might have been the outline of a lurid tale of espionage, a hint or two that his wife and he hadn't hit it off together, and the callous dismissal of the wife right at the end: what total could you evolve from that?

Yet in spite of his incommunicativeness she was breathlessly conscious of a latent, turbulent reservoir of passion which had been kept dammed for a long time. Or perhaps, in this cockeyed situation, she was letting her imagination stray too freely.

'Brothers and sisters?' she prompted.

'After the death of Hus,' he said in a slightly pedantic lecturer's voice, 'the Taborites founded a community where there was to be absolute social equality. No personal property, no power politics. Just mutual love and respect, and intensive Bible-reading. In essence the same as we're supposed to have now — apart from the Bible-reading.'

In a broad square, Maggie slowed and looked for some indication of their route. 'Thanks for the history. What about our immediate future — which way do we go?'

He leaned forward. 'I think . . . yes, that road for Budejovice.' As she drove on, he observed: 'My countrymen flatter the Russians.'

'Hm?'

'By supposing they can read. Tearing down the signposts.'

They went for some way in silence. The mountains remained obstinately distant, still no more than dark stains behind the nearer, gentler hills. A long, sprawling farm-house looked down from a slope, its arched gateway leading through an enclosing wall as though into a monastery.

Maggie said abruptly: 'You do have a proper exit visa, and all the rest of it?'

'And all the rest of it. All in order.'

The road went along the side of a valley. A field of grain shone golden below them, with a darker gash through it as though someone had swung a vast scythe ... or a Russian tank had perhaps crunched through on its way to some brutal rendezvous.

'Massacre rather than sacrifice,' Jan Melisek muttered, again to himself.

'What was that?'

He waved down towards the flattened blades.

'They don't even distinguish, the Russians,' he said. 'No selectivity. No ritual. Just smash everything in sight and hope you get the ones you're after. Saturation bombing of the spirit.'

'I still don't know what you're talking about.'

'About the harvest,' he said. 'And the kill dog.' The field of grain swung slowly below them. The road followed the leisurely curve of the valley. 'The barley dog, in some countries. It crops up all over Northern Europe, this belief in mischievous dwarfs working against the farmer. They're supposed to be able to disguise themselves as animals. When crops wave in the breeze, it means that the barley dog is running through them. You can't catch him until the harvest is almost ended. Then he runs until there's only one sheaf left, and he has to hide behind it. So you destroy the sheaf. Attack it with scythes — a ritual slaying to bring good luck to the harvest. Corner the symbolic enemy and exterminate him.'

'The kill dog.' Maggie shivered. 'That's

what gives me the creeps about your kind of work. It's all fascinating, I know, this digging up the past and relating it to history and making the pieces fit. Finding there's no such thing as progress and we're all barbarians at heart. But . . . you keep finding such horrible things, all the way back through the centuries.'

He nodded. 'Blood sacrifice of some kind, real or symbolic. More often real than symbolic.'

A narrow river ran beside the road, then opened out into a sequence of reedy lakes. For the first time Maggie became aware of the countryside as it really was — mellow, beautiful, melancholy — and not as mere distance to be covered quickly. She ought to have been allowed more time here, to get to know it, instead of having to race over it and away from it.

Jan Melisek said: 'And *your* kind of work?'

He was asking only out of politeness, of course. He didn't really care. Maggie kept it as terse as she could.

'Pre-Promotion Research,' she said. 'Market Research with a new slant. Our

Group does preliminary sampling — surveys almost at random, sometimes — and then we analyse what we've found. Instead of working along specified lines for specific firms, we explore the untapped possibilities. When we've studied the market and drawn our conclusions, we put up *our* ideas to manufacturers and sales organisations, instead of waiting for them to come to us. If they latch on, we offer facilities for full-scale investigation in depth.'

The cadences fell smoothly. Maggie knew from experience which patches of jargon to emphasise and which to deliver with skittish humour.

'You mean,' said her companion seriously, 'that you not only persuade people to buy something they would have been happy without, but you make a practice of showing manufacturers how to develop products which even *they* haven't considered foisting on the public?'

'Your English is very good,' said Maggie crossly, irrelevantly. 'But it's not very logical.'

'No? The logic in telling inventors to

invent something which nobody needs — '

'Look,' she said. 'Look. It's a matter of directing resources into the most rewarding channels. People don't have to buy what they genuinely don't want. They soon make up their own minds.'

'Do they? After such a conditioning — '

'Nobody can force them to buy what they don't want to buy.'

'But isn't that what you are doing? You collect answers to carefully phrased questions, listen to any emanations from the subconscious, and then tell your profiteers how they can most successfully appeal to hitherto unknown appetites — how to *create* appetites. And having created the appetite, you say that nobody needs to satisfy it if he doesn't wish to do so?'

Maggie was unprepared for a fast car that came snarling past them. She wavered into the middle of the road as though sucked in by the draught, braked, skidded a few yards and then straightened back on to course, angrier than ever.

'I know that right now it must seem pretty trivial to you,' she said. 'But in a free country, people have a free choice. It's our job to keep them informed, to give them a choice, to — '

'Tell me.' With maddening tact he had ignored the skid. 'What made you believe there was any scope for this sort of operation in Prague?'

It had been Mrs Chinnery's idea. 'Let's be first in the East!' Having read all about the thaw in Czechoslovakia and of the urgent need for business contacts with the West, Mrs Chinnery set one of her experts to finding out how Anglo-Czech trade stood at the moment, and what its immediate future was likely to be. Then someone had to be sent to Prague to make some preliminary inquiries. Czechoslovakia, Mrs Chinnery theorised, would need Market Research of quite a fresh kind. 'They won't have the ghost of a notion how to start after all those years of State oppression.' It might be a long-term project, or it might spark off sooner than one could predict.

Let the Chinnery Group be the pace-makers! What did the women of Czechoslovakia want? It was always the women who set the tempo. Study the shops; define the gaps between their standards and ours; quiz the people who work there, and the people who buy. Build up a complete picture. Then Mrs Chinnery's Export Assessment Division would advise British firms, liaise with Czechoslovak import officials, and get a retainer from whoever was prepared to pay.

Maggie had said dubiously: 'It sounds so . . .'

'Inspiring?' Mrs Chinnery suggested.

'Contrived.'

'Everything's contrived, dear. Only another word for skilful construction — and what's wrong with that?'

'Phoney, I mean.'

'It doesn't have to be,' Mrs Chinnery chided. 'Devise an *un*-phoney approach for us.'

Maggie did not tell Jan Melisek that she, too, had had doubts. Nor did she tell him of other fundamental doubts, further back. She was here under false pretences. If he visualised her as a smart, ruthless career girl, he was having hallucinations.

'Maggie'll go.' Oh yes, Maggie would go anywhere. They none of them knew how gawky and diffident she had once been, and how she still felt. It was this very diffidence which had made her the Maggie she supposedly was today. She played the brash pioneer even when it gave her the twitches. Jobs, interviews, challenges, tricky negotiations . . . you name it, Maggie tackles it. Like a sufferer from vertigo insisting on climbing a mountain to prove . . . well, to prove what?

Her mother had expressed resentful admiration. 'I don't know how you can do such things.' The resentment had, significantly, overshadowed the admiration.

A job in which she had perpetually to meet new people and deal off the cuff with new problems was the last thing Maggie had ever wanted: which was, basically, why she had taken it.

Now she said to this querulous stranger: 'All right, so the Prague thing fell through. But it had promise.'

'Had it? In this country we don't need telling what to buy. If it is there and we want it and can afford it, we buy. Otherwise we do without.'

'When there's a conflict of choice — '

'The only conflict is between what we want and what we can afford. The money we earn will go just so far. All the research and all the advertising in the world won't increase our spending.'

'Advertising lowers costs. People don't realise it, but it's true. Research makes marketing better for *everybody*, not just the seller.' It resonated with a tinny echo of Mrs Chinnery. Maggie changed tactics. 'What's so wonderful,' she demanded heatedly, 'about digging up a lot of axes and . . . well, combs and bronze girdles and whatnot . . . all that prehistoric junk? What's so marvellous about that, and so wrong about stimulating interest in the pleasures of the present?'

He looked at her. She refused to return his gaze. Quietly he said: 'I think you're right.'

'Delighted to hear it.'

'About the need for a drink,' he said. 'Shall we stop in this place ahead? I would like to buy you a glass of wine.'

It was a small town and a depressing one. The houses were even more scrofulous than those in Prague and lacked Prague's saving dignity — the fine bone structure which showed so nobly through the rotting flesh.

The restaurant was in a dusty square, facing an abandoned church. A tall crucifix remained by the church door, but the windows were shattered and from one of them projected a wooden chute, propped on one arm of the cross so that grain or potatoes could be poured into a store within the building.

Maggie hesitated on the step of the restaurant.

There was a smell of damp and decay. Huge iron-studded shutters, fastened back from the grimy windows, seemed to be held in place only by a couple of rusty hooks. One sagged drunkenly out over the street, ready to drop from its last hinge.

'If you would prefer us to cross the border first . . . '

'Let's have that glass of wine,' said Maggie. They went in.

The restaurant served no wine. Only beer or soda water: not even mineral water. They both chose beer.

A radio sputtered away in the corner. Three men, including the one who had brought the beer, stooped over it as though to drag better, more solid words out of it.

Jan Melisek slewed half round in his chair.

Maggie said: 'Professor . . . '

'Call me Jan. It's easier for an English tongue.'

'What's on the news? What are they saying?'

'Keep calm',' he translated. 'A clandestine station — but it's not trying to preach bloodshed.' He listened for a moment, then went on sketchily: ' 'The most ridiculous mockery in modern history is now entering its fifth day . . . a bungled putsch which will shame its perpetrators for a lifetime . . . ' Sit tight and show scorn — that's the general message. And now' — Jan frowned as he tried to catch the broadcast through an argument that had started around the radio set — 'they want . . . ' He put his head on one side. 'They're asking for students to come out into the country and help with the harvest. Polish troops have offered to help, but they're not acceptable. They ask . . . '

The metallic voice ceased abruptly.

The three men looked at one another and shrugged.

Jan said: 'Another one gone. The Russians have caught up with it.'

The men resumed their argument, louder now. Maggie felt that she was watching a foreign film without sub-titles.

One of them turned and spoke to Jan. His face darkened.

'Bad news?' asked Maggie.

'He asks if we are running away.'

'Well, we are.'

'You are going home, as is your right. But I . . . ' He looked out of the window as though debating whether to turn back along that road.

A lorry rumbled past. They all stiffened, wondering if it was an armoured car, perhaps the first of a convoy. The noise faded. Then there was the richer purr of a car, swinging round in the square and stopping.

The landlord muttered something to his cronies.

Jan said to Maggie: 'They've had quite a procession of refugees through here. They're wondering how long it will be allowed to go on.'

The door opened. Two men came in and stood just inside it, appraising the room. When they saw Jan they looked no farther. Their expressions did not change, but their arms and shoulders lost their tautness. Now they had found what they were looking for, they were at ease.

Maggie mumbled, as casually as possible: 'Trouble?'

In the same tone Jan replied: 'If there is trouble, you are to keep away. It is not your concern. Perhaps it would be better for you to leave now.'

'We shouldn't have stopped at all. You were right.'

The two men did not look especially menacing. They were middle-sized, dull

126

and matter-of-fact. Their job must be a fairly limited one: they had performed every move so often that it had become automatic. They had the sallow, sagging faces of assembly belt operatives.

One of them sauntered towards Jan's chair. The other moved only a few feet forward, covering the door but ready to snap into action if needed.

The three men by the silent radio were silent, too.

One of the newcomers spoke tersely to Jan.

The landlord wiped his hands on his sides and came out into the centre of the room. It was plain that he was asking them what they would like to eat or drink. He was waved aside.

Jan said something. The man beside him put one hand in his pocket and kept it there. In a casual tone Jan said across the table to Maggie: 'Strange. These creatures look very sure of themselves, but they can't really be sure enough. Why not notify the frontier guards if they want to hold me? Why not let them do the dirty work at the crossing point?'

Maggie looked at the man and tried not to flinch when he met her gaze. He was so nondescript, so undramatic. His eyes weren't cruel or crazy: just dead. The functionaries of fear ought somehow to have been more awe-inspiring than this.

The landlord growled something. Jan translated in his same unhurried voice: 'He wants to know if these two are friends of the Asiatics. Won't even call them Russians now — Asiatics!'

The man near Jan slammed one fist against the back of the chair, and shouted at the landlord.

One of the trio made an apologetic mumble and edged his way round the room. There was a brief hesitation; then the man at the door held it contemptuously open, letting him out.

Maggie sniffed. Someone clearing off home before the shooting started.

She wouldn't have minded clearing off home herself.

As though catching her thought in mid-air, Jan said: 'You must go. They have nothing against you.'

It was none of her business. She was a

foreigner, they would give her time to get clear before beating up this stranger, this Professor who meant nothing to her. She wouldn't have to watch them carting off the remains. A month from now she'd be busy on some new project, and she'd have forgotten all about him.

The two men were waiting, almost deferentially.

'I'll go when I choose.'

Good old bloody-minded Maggie, she said to herself. You fool. Get out while the going's good, like the nice gentleman says.

The apparent leader of the two tapped Jan on the shoulder and snapped an order. Jan rose slowly to his feet. Maggie tried to follow suit, but the man near the door came swiftly and unexpectedly round the table and pushed her down again.

She said: 'Now, look here . . . '

'Please,' said Jan. 'Let me deal with this in my own way. I can't fight back while you are here. Please go. Later I will find some way.'

'Such as?'

'Please go.' He added something in

129

Czech to the man by Maggie's chair. She watched as the man went away and opened the door once more. He stood there, waiting for her to leave.

Then he looked out across the square. Suddenly he tensed. His jaw dropped. He let out a furious yell. His companion rushed to the window and looked out. They both began to shout.

The landlord laughed. Jan laughed, but didn't trouble to offer Maggie an interpretation. Wildly, allowing no time for weighing up pros and cons, he launched himself at the door. The man staring out was knocked out into the street, and went down on hands and knees into the grit and dust.

The landlord bellowed something to Maggie. She ran. The man at the window was swinging round, his hand coming out of his pocket. He tried to grab her. She lashed out, caught him across the face and ran after Jan.

In the open air she caught a glimpse of a large black Tatra parked at the far kerb. Her own car was closer, but still seemed too far. She heard her pursuer's feet skid on the step; and the other man was getting up from the pavement.

As they raced past the window of the restaurant, the landlord leaned out. He might have been simply watching the chase. But as he put his weight against the heavy shutter, it came clear of its hook and swung outwards. The lower edge caught the first man on his left shoulder and threw him heavily out into the road. He screamed as he went down. The second man, still unsteady on his feet, couldn't stop himself. He walked straight into the metal crosspiece swinging loose from the shutter like a flail.

Jan reached the Renault and tugged at the door. 'Locked,' panted Maggie. She fumbled for the key, opened her door and plunged in, reaching out to free the other. Jan slid in beside her.

The car started at once, and she racketed it madly forward across the square. As they passed the Tatra she risked a glance at it.

The tyres were flat. She knew now what the supposed coward, slinking out, had had in mind.

Something hit the bonnet in front of her and screeched across it, scouring a furrow through the paint.

'That opening — down there, fast!' said Jan.

It was not until the muffled cough behind her was followed by another metallic shriek along the wing of the Renault that Maggie realised they were being shot at.

The road was narrow. For a moment she thought it was blocked. Then the dark grey shape of a tank, dead ahead, rocked to one side. They shot past it with an inch or so to spare.

'No,' breathed Maggie. She didn't know what she was denying, or who she was appealing to. She just felt sure that they were about to be blasted out of existence.

Jan craned back over the seat to see through the rear window. At the faint crack of another shot he laughed. 'They hit the tank. Weren't expecting it. That will take some explaining!'

'But when they have explained,' said Maggie, 'won't someone be able to phone to the frontier?'

'If they didn't arrange to stop us there in the first place, I don't see why they should do it now.'

They were clear of the town. Maggie looked up in her mirror every few seconds, but there was no sign of pursuit.

After a while, when she thought her breathing was under reasonable control, she said: 'Those men who helped us back there — won't they suffer for it?'

'I don't know.' He shook his head dazedly. 'I don't know at all. They were good Party members — tough ones, the real local dictators. The sort I'd have avoided normally. But when we got there, they were talking ... well ... ' He seemed to find difficulty in saying the word. 'Patriotically,' he came out with it. 'Cursing the Asiatics. Talking about standing firm. And they helped us — out of sheer defiance. It's ... I ... it's not the sort of thing that happened before. Never. It's all so new. Everything's upside-down.'

Again he shook his head, then lapsed into silence.

★ ★ ★

The car ate up the miles to the frontier. The road climbed steeply. The mountains were upon them now. Dark forests closed in on the road, shot through here and there with a stygian gleam of water.

Maggie wondered what would be waiting for them.

She said: 'Why were they after you, those two?'

'I don't know.'

'But you must . . . I mean, they wouldn't just show up out of the blue . . . '

'None of it fits,' he said abstractedly, as though it were some academic problem in which she could not possibly be interested.

'You're not smuggling anything out, are you?' she demanded. 'We're not going to be taken apart?'

'I trust not.'

'Look, if you *have* got anything hidden, I'd sooner know about it. Now.'

'I don't understand what could concern . . . *them*.'

'You don't sound too sure.'

'Today there's nothing in this country to be sure of.'

'What are you carrying?' asked Maggie resolutely.

'Some English money. Two hundred pounds.'

'You're not supposed to take it out of the country, are you?'

He grinned dourly. 'I was not supposed to bring it in, in the first place — not without handing it over to the State Bank. But I got it from my English publisher — Finch and Farrell, you know them? — and I didn't want Czech crowns in its place. Foreign currency is all you can use to buy foreign goods, a foreign car . . . '

'Like in that Tuzex place.'

'Just so.'

'It's so crazy. To admit that the biggest treat you can get in your high-minded democratic Communist state is the wherewithal to buy luxuries from the decadent West . . . I mean, isn't that an admission of failure anyway?'

'You are preaching to the converted, Miss Armitage.'

'Call me Maggie,' she said. 'It's easier for a Czech tongue.'

'Maggie.' He tried it over thoughtfully.

Then he said: 'Maggie, I tried to make you listen back in the restaurant. If there is trouble, you are to disown me. You kindly offered me a lift, but you know nothing about me or what I may be carrying.'

'So there *is* something else.'

'You hear me? If they stop me, then I take my cases off your car and you accept no responsibility for me.'

'What else?' She could be as stubborn as he was. 'What's the something you're not telling me about?'

'I don't see that it would mean anything to them.'

Maggie pulled in at the side of the road. There was nothing moving anywhere. Not a car in sight, not a prowling tank; nothing stirring in the woods.

She said: 'Come on. Tell me. Otherwise I may make you walk home.'

'Perhaps that would be better. I have no right — '

'Oh, do shut up. Look, I'll drive you over the border even if you're carrying plans for a new submarine and returned empties on a crate of American ammunition. But I want to *know*, that's all.'

He reached over the seat and groped for his brief-case from the back of the car. When it was open he drew out a piece of paper.

Maggie wondered for one sick moment if he really did have plans for an anti-missile missile or something. But what he handed to her was a clumsy sketch of some wobbly shapes like rectangles with knobs on. A few squiggly lines divided them from one another.

'Is that all?' She was relieved, yet deflated.

'That's all.'

He was an archaeologist, so she hazarded: 'They're ancient bodies, or something?'

'Bodies,' he said, 'perhaps.'

'Where?'

He slanted the sketch map. A name was scrawled in one corner, and there was an arrow, and a number that might have indicated a distance.

'It's baffling,' he said. 'That scrawl there could be Zdikov or Zdikovec.'

'They're close to each other?'

'Not very far apart. But enough to

make the exact location confusing.'

She studied the pencilled outlines again. 'Some burial ground?'

'It may be.'

'One of your pet Celtic burial grounds?' He had told her that much, and it seemed a fair guess.

'A very odd one, if it is.'

'You mean you don't know? But if it's so important . . . '

'I don't know that it is important. Or, rather, I don't know *why* it is.'

'But why are you carrying it? Where did it come from?'

'It came from . . . a friend.'

'And you didn't ask him what was so special about it?'

'No.'

'Why not?'

Jan said: 'He was dead.'

She looked from the map to his lowering brow. 'Let's get this straight. When you say dead — '

'I told you. Better for you to be rid of me. Drive a little closer to the frontier, then I get out and walk the rest of the way. On my own.'

'Balancing your bags on your head?'

She took the map from him. She, too, groped back over the seat, and hauled her large straw bag out.

'My grab-bag,' she explained.

'Please?'

'Never without it.' Eau-de-cologne tissue, a buckled reporter's notebook, some publicity brochures, a sexy paperback which had proved too boring for her to read more than half, a bar of chocolate and some crushed caramel wrappings, two handkerchiefs and a lipstick refill which she had bought a month ago, lost, and rediscovered. 'When in doubt,' she said, 'I dump everything in and catalogue it later. My grab-bag — because whatever else I'm doing or not doing, I grab this and take it along.'

She slid the map down so that only one creased corner was visible, and even then visible only if you knew what you were looking for. Then she tossed the creaking straw bag back where it came from, and drove on down the road.

'You think it's dangerous,' she marvelled, 'yet you don't know a thing about it or why it was given to you?'

'Not yet,' he said.

She glanced back over her shoulder. The bag had slipped down out of sight. It was a junk accumulator, and she had already torn three separate stockings on snags of the straw. It was light to carry; but now had acquired a sudden extra weight. It was like having a time bomb in with the groceries, ready to go off . . . when?

6

On his return Jan had made an official report on the Cambridge conference, knowing that Brok wanted it only in order to pick holes in it. They spent an hour together, and it was just as he had foreseen. Brok smiled his tusky yellow smile and made sharp verbal lunges and quick, insincerely apologetic withdrawals. He was as unctuous as any dentist, full of assurances that he didn't *mean* to hurt. Brok hated to be disliked, even by victims he had himself chosen.

Jan was not especially disturbed by Brok's interrogation. He was waiting for Veselka's questions.

The man was bound to want to know what had happened in England. Or what had not happened.

But days went by and there was no summons. It was insulting, more offhandedly contemptuous than anything so far. Jan hadn't been looking forward to confronting Veselka with the blunt announcement that he hadn't done what he had been asked and didn't ever intend to do anything. But he had been keyed up for it, and wanted to have it over and done with. The utter lack of interest was demoralising.

Perhaps that was the point. Veselka was biding his time. This was how they operated, these people — letting the string run out, then jerking it.

He telephoned Ladislav Adamec one evening and suggested a drink. Ladislav was sorry, but he was just on his way out.

Two evenings later, Jan tried again. Ladislav couldn't manage this time, either. He sounded evasive. Jan wondered if the name of Melisek was now on some unwritten list known to everyone but the accused: a list of people it was advisable to steer clear of. The years since 1948 had developed in most professional people a telepathic instinct for such things.

He found it hard to believe this of Ladislav.

And Blanka — did Blanka know something?

She seemed more contented than she had been before he went away. Something had happened in her job. She was vague about it — 'Same old responsibility, but a lot more of it.' Sometimes she came home late, but her grumbles were light-hearted. Occasionally a gleam of the old malice shone through, now directed at men other than himself. 'I tell you, there are some crafty types at the Radio who won't get away with their little schemes much longer.' He took it as a hopeful sign that she should want to confide in him, and tried to draw her out; but then she would close up and declare it was too complicated, or she was tired . . . or would simply wag her head and look very knowing.

Tentatively he suggested an evening out. They hadn't been out together for ages.

They went to a night club under Wenceslas Square. The food was good, but the hour's floor-show was dull. An almost bald charmer trailed a microphone on an interminable lead around the tables, simpering at two elderly ladies who found him irresistible, and loudly introducing a stream of girls dressed as feathered horses, feathered Mexicans or feathered poodles. The stream, if one watched closely enough, was made up of only four girls, who changed costumes and dashed on again, waggled for three minutes and dashed off again.

'I could do better than that myself,' said Blanka.

It was her announcement that the evening, like so many others in the past, was a flop. But on their way home she seemed to regret her abruptness and clung to his arm and kept glancing up at him and smiling.

Indoors, she said: 'Did those girls excite you?'

'No.'

'Not even the one with the big breasts, the one whose costume kept slipping?'

'I thought she was pitiful.'

'So did I.' Blanka began to undress. 'I still look better than that, don't I?'

They made love. She was sweating with impatience. In the middle of her paroxysm she twisted beneath him and brought up her knees in a mad contortion. She

144

held him trapped while her hands robbed him of breath and tortured him until it was over.

'Where did you learn *that* one?'

He gasped it out as a rueful joke, but when she laughed it wasn't at the joke but at some obscene triumph of her own.

The following evening she was an hour later than he getting home. 'I've been looking in the shops. Queues for Christmas already.'

Later she tapped on the door of the sitting-room and asked if he was very busy. He invited her in, and they sat down companionably. He didn't understand quite why they were getting on so much better; but he wasn't going to be foolishly hypercritical.

They had a glass of wine each. Blanka asked what things had been like at the Institute since he came back. She brought up the names of some of his colleagues. A few she had met in those days when he had tried to keep up some kind of social life. There were others he couldn't recall having even mentioned to her.

It was pleasant to chat like this, though,

without strain. Until he was plucked by an uneasy suspicion. He stopped in mid-sentence and said:

'Why do you want to know all this?'

'I tell you about *my* work.'

'Not very much.'

'Well, it's not as interesting as yours.' She pouted. 'I thought you'd *like* me to ask about what you do.'

From then on he phrased everything in the most non-committal way, telling anecdotes in favour of men he liked, and praising their work. He found that if he had nothing discreditable to tell her she soon lost interest.

Shortly before Christmas he met Ladislav in the entrance to the Institute, and insisted they must have a drink that evening. The younger man was awkward and reluctant, but equally reluctant to dodge too blatantly. They arranged to meet in the usual place.

* * *

The moment he reached the kavarna he saw that Ladislav had been drinking already. Not just in the few minutes he had probably been here, but before that. At home, alone? It wasn't like him.

Jan sat down. 'Haven't seen much of you lately.'

'I've been up to the eyes in work.'

'I thought you'd been avoiding me.'

'What?' Ladislav let out a noisy laugh. 'Good heavens, what gave you that idea? Just that I've been away, that's all. Doing some research in Sumava.'

Jan was puzzled. Ladislav was a Slavonic specialist and his natural territory was the Chodsko area, the only ethno-graphically preserved Slav whole.

'Sumava?' he said. 'Looking for sports and strays?'

'Shop talk.' Ladislav ventured a reproving grin, but it came out unconvincingly. He added, as though to get it over with: 'Incidentally, I'm expecting to go to Paris some time in the New Year.'

'They're letting you out?'

Ladislav was unmarried. His parents were dead. It was rare for such a man to be allowed out of the country on his own, with no hostages to guarantee his return.

Having got this bit of news off his chest, Ladislav acquired a certain drunken swagger. He began to ask Jan's advice, as an old hand. 'When you're out there, how careful do you have to be about what you say — about things here, I mean?'

'Use your own judgement.'

'Yes, but . . . I mean, do they ask a lot of questions?'

'If they do, you don't have to answer them.'

'How much do *you* let yourself go, when you're abroad?'

Jan tried to decide whether the question was calculated or blunderingly innocent.

You learned not to take risks. Even with a trusted friend . . . a friend who had been trusted until now. He said: 'I always stick to the subject in hand.'

'You don't think foreigners ought to be told what it's really like? Don't let them know the truth?'

At any other time Jan would have accepted the cue to discuss the changing face of truth, periodically reshaped by the authorities, rather like a political fashion parade. Now he was cautious. Ladislav sounded like an apprentice agent-provocateur.

All a matter of mistaken emphasis, he told himself.

But once you had started suspecting, you went on. In the sullen climate of treachery that had blanketed the country for so long, you were alert for the familiar symptoms. Once the smell of it was there, like an insidious dampness in your clothes, you couldn't stop sniffing at it.

He said: 'What does Veselka want you to do for him in Paris?'

It was a wild shot, and he felt sick when he saw what an incontestable hit he had scored. Ladislav gulped horribly on his drink, waved one hand to indicate that he was all right, and converted the wave into a demand for the waiter to come and bring more beer.

'Well?' said Jan.

'Sorry. Went down the wrong way. What was that?'

'Veselka,' said Jan. 'You've been approached. You've agreed. You must have done, or you wouldn't be allowed out.'

'I don't have to put up with Brok any

more. D'you understand? Brok is going to be put in his place . . . '

Jan heard an unsettling echo of Blanka prophesying doom for enemies in the Radio. He shut it out, knowing it would return to torment him.

'Veselka,' he said again.

'Jan . . . we've been friends for a long time, you and I. You've understood a lot. Friends — right?'

'You're less careful in your choice of friends than you used to be.'

'Damn it, doing things their way — it's the only way. If you want anything at all out of life — '

'You think they care what you want?'

Ladislav had ordered a large vodka. He tipped half of it back. 'Play them along, or else you never get anywhere.'

'Depends where you want to get. And whether you can bear to live with yourself when you get there.'

'I know what I'm doing.'

'Veselka,' Jan hammered on remorselessly.

'All right, all right. I was approached. That may have been his name.'

'You know it was.'

'There are worse things.'

'Name some.'

'Jan, you don't know — '

'No, I don't. What deal was proposed? A jaunt to Sumava, a week in Paris . . . in exchange for what?'

'Jan.' Ladislav's maudlin wail cracked farcically into a hiccup. 'Maybe' — he fought to get his breath back, and the words simmered for even longer than usual — 'he . . . maybe . . . Brok isn't as secure as he likes to think.'

The echo taunted Jan again. He blazed: 'You seriously think they'll get rid of Brok for you? Have you got it in writing? What's the deal — do they want you to assassinate de Gaulle?'

'Look. Look.' Ladislav struggled, and managed to repeat: 'L-look. Don't get so damned high and mighty. You ought to be glad . . . grateful.'

'Ought I?'

'You know what he wanted me to do at first? He told me to concentrate on *you*.'

'Did he? Did he, indeed?'

'But I didn't.' Ladislav was maudlin,

eager, collapsing. 'You know I didn't. I never hung round you and asked questions, did I? Never tried to incriminate you?'

'I thought he'd forgotten me,' said Jan.

'Forgotten? Oh, don't ever count on that.' The young man's eyes were bleary and haunted. 'He never forgets anyone. There was a lecturer in the Carolinum he'd got a grudge against. Wanted to know what I could tell him. On and on and on — wouldn't leave it alone. And there was this man from Vimperk, a reporter, the one I had to talk to while I was supposed to be working in Sumava. I had to lead him on and listen and remember every word, and pass it on. I had to do it. He was storing something up against the man. I don't know where it was all leading, or what'll happen. Maybe,' he comforted himself, 'nothing at all.'

'A reporter?'

'It was better than having to spy on *you*, wasn't it? When he took me off you and sent me off to concentrate on this other man, I kept everything as woolly as possible. Nothing the fellow said was — '

'Lada.' Jan cut him short. 'Why did Veselka give me up so easily, when he's so determined in other directions?'

Ladislav's hand shook on his glass. He drank, and fought off another hiccup. 'I couldn't very well ask him that, could I?'

'But you know.'

'Jan, I oughtn't to talk about it.'

'Go on.'

'I swear to you, I didn't know she was involved.'

'It's all right. It's no news to me.' And that, really, was true.

'She's been protecting you. You do know that?'

'Nice of her,' said Jan. 'Loyal of her. What more can a husband ask?'

'She told him she didn't want you hounded. You've got to believe that, Jan.'

'Oh, I believe it. She's got a very sensitive conscience.'

'He's crazy about her.' Ladislav slurred his words more than ever, as though to rob them of any hurtfully sharp edges. 'He does what she says. For the time being, anyway.'

'For the time being.'

' 'But we can always come back to him.' That's what he said to me, about you. 'We can always come back to him when the time's right.' '

'So he hasn't given me up as a bad job.'

'I told you. He never forgets anyone. The stuff he already knew about that reporter — scores of insignificant little details, trivial stuff from years back. 'I never forget.' I can hear him saying it.'

Jan looked at his friend's empty glass. He was doubtful of the wisdom of refilling it. Ladislav himself appeared to have doubts. He was breathing in a calculated, sobering rhythm. After a while he forced words out:

'Maybe it's all over now.'

'Why should it be?'

'There are so many things going on. Men like that . . . they may soon be out of a job.'

Jan snorted mirthlessly. 'All the secret police on pension? I don't think the economy can afford it.'

'But things are happening. There's something going on in the Praesidium.

Big reforms, they say. I've heard the Central Committee has been in session for days on end.'

'Yes,' said Jan. 'And brother Brezhnev dropped in a few days ago just to make it clear how far the reforms would be allowed to go. So don't think we're all going to live happily ever after.'

'It can't get worse than it used to be,' said Ladislav fervently. 'It's got to get better.'

The affirmation seemed to cheer him up. He had got the shabby story off his chest, topped it off with an incantation, and now he was cleansed.

They left. Jan offered to walk home with Ladislav, but was relieved when he was waved aside. Ladislav went off at a steady gait. Jan could only hope that his eventual hangover would not precipitate a relapse into despair and self-pity.

When they had parted, he began to think not of Ladislav but of himself. And of Blanka.

It was impossible. All of it. Filthy, warped, sickening and impossible.

He thought of Veselka gloating.

Veselka, perverse and sadistic, with Blanka as a willing partner.

She's been protecting you . . . didn't want you hounded.

Blanka was very subdued as he entered the flat. She knew who he had met. That hadn't kept her noticeably withdrawn and quiet in the past.

She said only: 'Had a good gossip?'

'You could call it that.'

She fussed with something at the back of the kitchen cupboard. 'Men are much worse than women.'

'Some men certainly like collecting it,' he agreed, 'from all conceivable sources.'

'You'd like a cup of coffee?'

He said: 'Where were you on Tuesday evening? And last night? You were late. Very late.'

'I've told you. It's a new job.'

'Tell me. Tell me a lot more.'

'I can't. There are security elements. If I have to work late — '

'Reporting,' he said. 'Poking and prying all day long, and then going off to snigger over it all with Veselka.'

'You're drunk.'

'No.'

'Somebody has been drunk this evening, then.'

'Tell me about Veselka.' He had uttered the name so often this evening that it was becoming unreal. Nobody could possibly be called Veselka.

Blanka swung towards him. For a moment there might have been a choice. She might have chosen the way of defiance and denial. But suddenly she cried: 'What are *you* complaining about? Don't you like things quiet and comfortable, the way they are?'

'No,' he said; 'not the way they are.'

'You don't want to shelter behind a woman's skirts?'

'I don't trust — '

'You're the only one, then. In my job I'm trusted. It won't do you any harm to have a wife who's trusted, will it? Trusted . . . protected.'

He thought of her prying and probing. What a chance to repay old scores! Perhaps, in spite of her talk of sheltering him, he was on her schedule. If Veselka wanted to know where he was vulnerable,

Blanka was the one to tell him. Didn't she know how she was being used?

Perhaps she thought she was in control. Ladislav had said Veselka was infatuated with her.

He said: 'I won't have it.'

'You're getting jealous?' She was delighted.

'It's got to stop. Whatever job you're doing for that man, it stops now.'

'And he turns his attentions to you again?'

'You can't go on living here with me if — '

'Oh, but I can. I am employed, I have the same rights as you. And I have influence.' She giggled. 'If anyone leaves, it'll be you.'

His impulse was to drag out his old trunk, throw clothes into it and go now so that there should be no mistake. But it was too histrionic. He wasn't made that way. And to leave Blanka to the mess in which she would inevitably find herself . . .

Absurd that he should feel compassion rather than hatred. Would he never be

158

able to hate as easily as she did?

'Well?' she said.

'I've got to think,' he temporised.

'Yes. Do think. Jan' — she was smugly sure of herself, sure enough to tell him that he existed only on sufferance — 'we can get along all right. You get on with your work, I get on with mine. We're both adults. It's only a job.'

'Only a job?' he echoed derisively.

'We're comfortable enough here, aren't we? Jan, I don't want you to go.' When he tried to reply, she quickly said: 'Do think about it, Jan.'

★　★　★

The following day was confused by a conference called by Brok. It was purposeless, and could have been provoked only by some idea that they ought to indulge in *some* sort of ritual before Christmas, and that a few threats ought to be planted ready for the New Year. Nothing of any consequence was said, and there was little need to listen.

But it was hard to concentrate on

anything else. Blanka, said Jan to himself, a hundred times during the morning. Blanka. It led nowhere. Veselka. Blanka and Veselka. Stupid bitch. Did she really imagine . . . ?

He should have thrown her out last night — thrown her out, literally, bodily. Cause a scandal, smash up everything for both of them. Let Veselka do his worst. Better than living a lie.

But living a lie had become a stoical habit.

When he left the Institute late that afternoon he walked for more than an hour. There had to be a way of dealing with this noisome business so that some dignity could still remain for Blanka and himself.

He could almost hear Veselka's sly laughter.

Walking and walking, pounding away at the problem inside his head — and when he entered the gloomy hall of the block of flats he had still made no decision.

Automatically he went to the row of deep grey metal letter-boxes. Just below the rim of the Melisek box there appeared to be a large envelope. He got out his key and opened the box. There was no envelope, but a folded sheet of cartridge paper. In the feeble light at the foot of the stairs he could make out only a few pencilled shapes and a name scrawled in one corner. There was no explanatory note with it.

Jan refolded the sheet and dropped it into his brief-case. He was in no mood to puzzle over such things now.

He climbed the stairs.

Of course she hadn't admitted — not in so many words — anything about having an actual affair with Veselka.

Yes, she had. It was in every glance and movement. She had wanted him to know.

The door of the neighbouring flat opened as he reached the last few steps. Mrs Fried came out and waited for him under the alcove with its statue of St John Nepomuk. Back in the Stalinist years, the flats committee had earnestly debated whether or not to take down the statue and demolish it. No firm decision had ever been reached.

Nobody put sprigs of flowers there any more; but the statue itself remained.

Mrs Fried said: 'You've missed a caller, Professor. He seemed very anxious to see you. He went on ringing and ringing the bell.'

'I'm sorry if you were disturbed.'

'Not at all, not at all.' She was a good-hearted woman, but she did like the privilege of a little grumble. 'But hearing the ringing, I came out.'

'Did he leave a message?'

'Not with me,' said Mrs Fried regretfully. 'I told Mrs Meliskova when she came in, a few minutes ago,' she added.

Jan put his key in the door. Reluctant to let the topic slide away, Mrs Fried contributed further information: 'He was a youngish man. Very pale. Oh, and he stammered a little. Well, not what you'd rightly call a stammer, but — '

'Yes,' said Jan. 'Thank you, yes. I know who you mean. A colleague of mine from the Institute.'

'Nothing serious, then?'

'Nothing,' said Jan firmly. 'He works

hard, and worries too much over detail, that's all.'

He nodded politely, and went in.

Blanka had been waiting for him. He could tell she was tensed, expectant; and he had no doubt that she had been rehearsing splendid, floridly defiant speeches.

He put his brief-case down. Marking time, he said: 'I gather Ladislav has been here.'

'Oh, him.'

'He seems to have been worried about something.'

'Is that all you can think of?'

He felt a childish urge to be just as wayward and difficult as she habitually was. She was braced for a row. Let her wait.

He went to the telephone.

'You don't want to talk to him now.' Blanka's sharpness was surprising even for her.

'May as well find out what he wanted.'

'Jan, don't.'

He stared, then said: 'Afraid he's got something special to tell me?'

'What could he have . . . ?'

'A bit more about your services to the State, maybe.'

'Jan.' She was shouting now; and she was scared. 'I wouldn't. Leave Adamec alone.'

Jan dialled. Blanka advanced as though to snatch the phone from him. He held it firmly.

There was no reply.

When he put the receiver down, she said: 'There. Are you satisfied?'

'What's going on?'

'I don't know. Adamec is nothing to do with me. Jan, I thought — '

'I want to know more about this.'

There was nothing to be alarmed about. Mrs Fried might have thought the young man looked worried, but he often looked like that. If he were as drunk as he had been at that last meeting, he could well have gone on and on ringing the doorbell, muzzily frustrated at not finding Jan there to listen to further confessions.

But Mrs Fried had said nothing about his being drunk, and she was not the sort of woman to miss a symptom like that.

'Jan,' Blanka wailed, 'we've got to talk.'

'Yes. We have. I won't be long.'

He went out. Postponing the next clash?

No. He was genuinely perturbed. Not so much by Mrs Fried as by Blanka. She had been too anxious to obliterate Ladislav from his mind.

He walked up the hill to the kavarna, just in case Ladislav had blearily settled himself there. But there was no sign of him. Jan walked on, under the pale lights of the castle courtyards, and down into the shadows of the Little Quarter.

The room in which Ladislav lived was on a second storey above an inner courtyard. As a rule it was badly lit save for what glow seeped down from windows along the narrow balconies running round three sides of the yard. This evening, however, there was a blaze of brightness against one wall.

The headlamps of a police car were beamed on the huddle of tall dustbins, jaggedly festooned at the moment with some broken railings. Above, hazier in the diffused light, there was a gap in the rail of the second balcony.

Crumpled over the dustbins, with one broken rail disappearing into the darkly spreading pulp of his neck, was what was left of Ladislav Adamec.

7

An accident. That was the official verdict. Jan might wonder if there had been instructions from elsewhere that this was how the police were to treat the matter; but it would do him no good to wonder out loud.

An accident. Nobody in the other flats had heard anything apart from the crash. From behind double windows, closed against the night cold, it had sounded like the usual clatter of the dustbins, even if a bit rowdier than normal. It was some time before a woman, seeing the broken rail, had gone down to investigate.

An accident. All the balcony railings were old and faulty. Why had this not been reported to the District Enterprise of Housing Economy? But it had, over and over again. Nothing had been done. There was no incentive; no sense of urgency; no sense of responsibility.

'An accident,' said Jan to Blanka. Then

he said: 'Now let's have the truth.'

'You don't think *I* had anything to do with it?'

'You knew something. You knew what was going to happen to Lada.'

'Jan, no. I didn't. I swear I didn't.'

'You knew he had been here. Tell me — I'm going to find out, I promise you — did you phone Veselka and tell him, before I got back?'

'No.' She was shaking. 'He was nothing to do with me. They were . . . on to him already.'

'Why?'

'I don't know. I don't know.'

'He was one of your lot. He'd been suborned, just like you. So what went wrong: why did he have to be murdered?'

'It was an accident. You saw for yourself — '

'Yes. I saw for myself. And I still want to know: why did he have to be eliminated?'

'Jan, you don't understand — '

'I understand. I understand that you've been working in the Radio for Veselka. I understand you've been sleeping with

168

him. I understand — '

'Who says so?' It was the joyful anguish he knew of old.

'I've only to look at you. And listen to you.'

'But you're not going to stir up trouble, now, are you? You've been doing some thinking.' She was gabbling the words out, steering the argument the way she wanted it to go. 'Very wise. Make a fuss, and the pressure's on you again, isn't it? So you're going to be very clever and keep very quiet — '

He hit her. She reeled back against the table. He hit her again so that she blundered on against the wall. As she put her hand up to her face she smiled.

'Jan, I'm sorry, but it's been for the best. Truly it has.' She was in pain, yet was positively cooing.

He said: 'I still want to know. What turned the vultures on Ladislav?'

'How should I know? Does it matter now? There isn't anything anyone can do. I expect he was . . . well, unreliable. In some way. I don't know.'

'Unreliable?' Jan let fly. 'And what

about you, then? Doesn't Veselka know how unsafe you are — how utterly incapable of keeping your mouth shut?'

'He trusts me.'

'So besotted with you he can't see what a liability he's got on his hands? All right, he wants the latest dirt from the Radio, and it's a job you love. But does the muck get filtered exclusively to him?'

'Jan, I'm telling you, if it weren't for me — '

'You can't keep anything to yourself. You want the world to know what a special, knowing little bitch you are. The man must be mad.'

'He's mad about me,' she goaded, wanting to be hit again. And then she really expected that he would make love to her.

Love: an assault, a debasement, each time something vicious and exciting. But when the swift excitement was over, then what?

She waited for him to make a move.

Implacably he said: 'So you don't know why Lada was killed?'

'How many more times?'

Her exhaustion wasn't feigned. She really didn't know, and she wasn't going to be any help to him. He had only guesswork to go on. Veselka's men must have followed Ladislav here. Perhaps this hadn't dawned on the young man until he went downstairs after trying to make himself heard. Looking out from the dark entrance he must have seen someone lurking across the street, or at any rate been alarmed enough to squash the sketch hurriedly into Jan's letter-box before emerging.

There was no way now of being sure; but this pattern made sense. Which was more than the map did.

Ladislav had been murdered because of those scribbles on a sheet of cartridge? It was out of all proportion. Jan had covertly studied the map and wanted more time, when he was sure of being alone. The sketch appeared to represent crude wall-paintings, or just conceivably a simple burial ground — in Southern Bohemia? But not Celtic. Or was it? Was it a unique discovery which Lada had wanted to pass on?

Perhaps the killing was, confusingly, separate.

'Well, Jan?' It was Blanka, coaxing.

'I'm staying,' he said.

'I'm so glad.' She could have been a hostess not wanting him to leave too soon. 'I knew you'd be sensible.'

'Staying on,' he said, 'until I find out what happened to Lada. And what's happening to you.'

'Jan, that's not what I meant.'

'It's what I mean, though.'

'We can't go on . . . distrusting each other.'

She was incredible. Sincere, plaintive and incredible.

He said: 'Blanka, you still don't know what you're mixed up in.'

There were tears in her eyes. She cried readily, cathartically.

'Jan, I can't expect you to want me. Not feeling the way you do.' It was his fault and not hers that he felt the way he did. 'Don't think I'm asking for anything. I don't blame you — really I don't — even if you hate me.' She was willing him to give her the hot satisfaction of being hated. 'Can't we leave it at that, and . . . well, *try?*' And then: 'For the time being, anyway?'

'And stop asking awkward questions?' he prompted.

'For both our sakes.'

'And for the sake of Lada's memory?'

'Jan, I swear to you I'd no idea. About him, I mean. If I'd known — '

'What would you have done?'

'Why can't you stop? I had nothing to do with him. I'd never have taken any part in . . . in anything of that kind. Never.'

'If they'd asked you . . . '

'They didn't. They didn't.'

'But if they had, and you hadn't wanted to, and you'd still been forced? If they'd insisted?'

'Jan, stop it. Stop it, stop it, stop it.'

She was still crying. It was getting worse. Her sobs became long-drawn-out rasps in her throat. She breathed harshly, choked, and the sobs took on a slower yet more hysterical rhythm.

'Now you're beginning to get frightened,' he said. 'About time, too.'

He had to give her half a tumbler of vodka to numb the gasping frenzy. Then he put her to bed. She groped for him, wanting him to come in with her and into her.

He waited until he was sure she was asleep, and then went and lay on his bed for hours before undressing and finally going off to sleep himself.

Thousands of couples lived out mutually antipathetic marriages. Petty deceits, shifty compromises, drab acceptance of the unacceptable. In a way it might be more tolerable than the past had been. Now he was fully conscious, forewarned, always on his guard: he had no illusions and so was safer.

The safety of being so far down that there was no further to fall . . .

★　★　★

In January the rumours came true. The impossible began to work out its destiny. Men and women who had never been interested in politics, or had found it safer to show no interest, whispered; then spoke

174

out; then argued in streets and restaurants, in trams and in the shops.

Novotny had been removed from his post of First Secretary.

It was all over so smoothly, without bloodshed and without demonstrations, that it seemed too good to be true. And even if it were true, would what followed be any different?

Who had ever heard of this man Dubcek before?

A Slovak. Well . . .

Whispers . . . muttering . . . look, is something really going to happen?

Socialism with a human face?

'Ridiculous,' a man would mumble. Then he would shout it, across a table in a bar. And the argument would start, and someone would say 'Shush!' in an agony of waiting for the S.T.B. to appear.

The sense of freedom was heady, and dangerous.

It wouldn't work. Couldn't work.

Censorship was to be abolished.

Don't believe it.

Yet there was this euphoria. A new spirit at the top and in the streets and offices and shops and factories.

And in the middle?

There were men who would never willingly relinquish their sinecures. The time-servers: could you really believe they would change, learn an honest trade, disappear to make way for new men? In the end it must somehow be business as usual, under Dubcek or anybody else.

And what were the secret police doing all this time, with their files and their cells and their specialised techniques? Disbanding themselves? Attending agricultural colleges or taking up engineering apprenticeships?

In February, President Novotny came out into the open with a plea to factory workers to rally behind him in defence of all they had sought to achieve. A few weeks later he ceased even to be President.

Svoboda . . . Freedom.

'Ah, my dear Melisek,' Brok stopped Jan in the corridor. 'My dear fellow, things going well?' Brok was still here, anyway, and would go on being here.

'Well enough.'

'A wonderful feeling, yes?' Brok's expansive wave might have been designed to draw attention to a magnificent view seen from a bright hilltop. 'Now perhaps we can work in sunshine instead of groping through the fog. Isn't that how it strikes you, my dear fellow?'

'Things look better.'

'We have been waiting so long for this, people like you and me.' Brok clenched his right hand on Jan's left arm. They walked slowly along the corridor. 'I must have a chat with you one day soon. Now we have the opportunity, there are many problems I'd like to see cleared up. We can talk freely at last. There are wrongs which ought to be set right.'

'Indeed?'

'Zidek. I've always worried about poor Zidek.'

Hardly surprising, thought Jan. It was Brok who had informed on Zidek — not because there was anything to inform about, but because in a purge decreed of intellectual dissidents there had by the law of averages to be at least one scapegoat in the Institute, and the nomination of one such had fallen to Brok. He had chosen Zidek.

Nobody had protested. Nobody had admitted to being perplexed by the hows and whys. If a plague passed by your door, you didn't go out and plead with it to come back and afflict you, too. Let the victim be quietly removed without breathing on you.

'They were unsettling times,' said Brok. 'Now we can say what we feel, I'm determined to have Zidek rehabilitated.'

Jan felt glad for Zidek's sake. But he wanted to shake Brok's hand off his sleeve.

He had rarely done more than skim through newspapers. When they consisted of no more than amplified handouts and proclamations, there had been no point in wasting time on them. Now, like everyone else, he was eager to read what was being said.

It won't work. Can't work.

Yet it seemed to be working. There was a gaiety even in criticism. Demands on the new Government came in a mighty tide — but a boisterous, invigorating tide.

One evening he bought *Vecerni Praha* on the way home, and saw the announcement of a new sequence of reforms, including the phasing out of the secret police. He hoped it would make good reading for Veselka over his supper.

When he got in, the flat was silent. For a moment he was stricken, visualising Blanka plotting somewhere with Veselka. Or perhaps they were busily tearing up incriminating documents. A gruesomely farcical picture.

Then he noticed that the door to the sitting-room was ajar. Although there was still no sound, he knew Blanka was in there.

'Is that you, Jan?'

He walked into the sitting-room. She was lying face down, naked, on the divan.

'You're here,' she sighed.

Her body was plump, smooth and desirable. And she was an utter stranger.

'Jan,' she said. 'Make it all right. Please.'

Her arm waved vaguely out into the room. There was a leather belt lying coiled on the table.

'Please, Jan, make it all right.'

A ripple of anticipation started in her shoulders and ran down her back. He touched the belt as though it were a snake which might rear up at him. She heard the faint click of the buckle against the table, and gave a little moan.

'Oh, this is ridiculous.' He swept the belt away with the back of his hand.

'Jan . . . ' It was a shivering wail. Blanka turned over, her arms and legs spread imploringly. 'Can't you . . . couldn't you . . . '

He made love to her, and it was fine; but not what she had really been wanting.

Afterwards there was the familiar emptiness. There ought to be an after-math of affection and warm laughter. Somehow there ought to be a lot of laughter, because the whole thing ought to have been mad and funny and sweet. Blanka's masochistic intensity would never let it be that way.

So, he thought as they dressed, he had given in. One step. And then another would be demanded of him.

After what you know about her, you took her back? He could imagine some invisible inquisitor asking in a tone of disbelief how he could have done it. No pride? Lust winning in the end? No . . . not lust: quiet desperation. Not the satisfying of an appetite but the hope that it will lead to affection, to a rekindling . . . Oh, it's failed a hundred times already, but you keep hoping that the joining of your bodies will work this time — that it won't stop there, but that the warmth will continue and not die away this time.

Blanka said: 'What are you thinking?'

There was nothing he could say to that.

'Jan . . . I'm not going to work for that man any more.'

'You've fallen out?'

'I don't like the way things are going.'

'Most people in the country are very pleased with the way things are going.'

'That's what I mean. No, what I mean is, I think he's going to do something silly. He thinks he can still go on the old way, waiting for a chance, and . . . Jan, there won't be a swing back, will there?'

'He's scared?' said Jan. 'Or you're scared?'

'I don't want to be mixed up in anything. I only did what I was told. It was purely routine, it wasn't anything awful. I don't want — '

'Blanka,' he said gently, 'there's no need to go on.' She was patting her hair slowly and sadly in the mirror, watching his reflection from an angle. 'I understand,' he said.

'Do you, Jan? Do you really? If you really think I *could* give up that part of the job — if you want me to, if that's what you think . . . '

Yes, he understood.

And later, after they had eaten, she said in a level, reasonable voice: 'I can't expect you to want me. I know it won't ever be the same, not after everything that's happened.'

But it was just what she did expect. Her nude, fervid welcome of him this evening had been meant to prove something.

She had nobly given up Veselka. She expected an adequate reward.

A few days later, when Jan asked about her job in the Radio and how she had dealt with Veselka, she said: 'Jan, I'm not the only one. He can't pick on all of us because we've . . . well, backed out. I don't have to bother about him. We don't have to mention him ever again.'

But without even bringing up Veselka's name, Jan knew they would implicitly be talking about him for a long time yet.

★   ★   ★

Public brains-trusts were becoming as popular as football matches or pop music festivals. Dance-halls and factories were the scenes of soul-searching debates and meetings. 'Open the door' — unthinkably, it was the politicians themselves who took the floor and faced their critics. Philosophers and sociologists joined them on a dozen platforms. Factory workers, students, tram-conductors . . . suddenly everybody was talking.

Jan was invited to appear with a group in the Municipal House. In spite of the spaciousness of the Smetana Hall, there were hundreds of young people still waiting outside when the session began.

In the Central Committee, the deposed Novotny was allowed to make a long speech. 'Negative forces in this country are being activated . . . ' They let him ramble on, but the constant ripples of laughter were not encouraging.

A week later Brok approached Jan, holding a sheet of paper.

'I'm sure you would like to add your signature to *this*, my dear Melisek.'

It was a denunciatory letter addressed to the ex-President of the Republic, similar in tone to an open letter already sent by historians from the Academy of Sciences. There was already a column of signatures.

'We all feel it's time we spoke out,' said Brok, 'in support of our colleagues.'

'I don't agree.'

Brok looked surprised. 'But surely you are in sympathy with — '

'He's down,' said Jan. 'Leave him.'

'After the monstrous oppression of his regime? After all we were made to suffer?' Brok let out his breath in an indignant hiss, then breathed in more thoughtfully. 'You're not . . . you don't think there might be a chance of his reasserting himself — of coming back? Is that why you're chary of signing?'

'No. Whether he comes back or stays where he is, it makes no difference. Put your energy into supporting the new people; never mind about kicking the old.'

Brok said: 'But if we are to learn from our past errors . . . '

He went on at great length, while Jan thought of Blanka and his own past errors, and wondered whether, however much one might learn, there was the slightest chance of applying that learning and watching it work out as it should.

★ ★ ★

Blanka said: 'It's this flat. It has too many memories, hasn't it?'

'I don't fancy looking for another one.'

'Not yet, of course. Not right away. But it would do us good to have a holiday. Don't you think so? To go off somewhere, just for a week or so. It's easy now. We can travel where we like, when we like. You can get visas without question.'

'Yes.' Jan turned the idea over in his mind.

'I suppose it would be silly to talk of having a second honeymoon.' Blanka's eyelids closed and opened very slowly, demurely.

She dared him to say that it was silly.

Jan said: 'Let's have a week in Vienna.'

'Oh. I was thinking — '

'We can drive there. Take our time, see the country on the way.' He could see she wanted to argue, but it would mean changing the mood she had thought herself into. He went on 'Perhaps in August, when I've more time, we could go to England.'

'That's what I thought you'd want anyway.'

'Let's try Vienna first.'

She was still not sure how to react to this. He applied for visas and made a hotel booking before she could become too querulous. If she challenged him, saying that he didn't want her to come to England with him, there was bound to be a row. He dreaded the thought of her in England.

And yet he was still trying to pretend that their marriage could be made to work?

They went to Vienna.

Blanka set about being noisily gay. She wanted to go on the big wheel and on swings, and throw her legs up in the air. She got drunk easily, as she hadn't got drunk since those incidents in the past.

One evening she knocked a glass of wine across the floor in a restaurant, and howled with laughter, as though nothing like this had ever happened in the world before.

'Shall we stay here?' she cried. 'Never go back? Isn't that what you've always wanted?'

'I don't think so.' Jan realised that he hadn't thought of such a thing since travel restrictions had been eased. Hadn't thought of it, in fact, since that day outside Orford. 'No, when it comes down to it I don't think I'd ever want to . . . well, not go back. Not ever go back.'

'After all you've told me about England — '

'This isn't England.'

'Let's go and settle there, then,' she cried recklessly. 'There's nothing to stop us now. Let's go while we still have the chance.'

'The chance?' In her moist eyes he saw the old, bragging streak. 'What are you trying to say?'

'Not trying. Don't have to try. Just saying.' Her loosely waving arm threatened peril to a fresh glass. 'Let's go, that's what I'm saying. Just in case.'

'Look,' he said: 'do you *know* something?'

'Don't know a thing.' She was happily muzzy, still hugging herself like a pregnant woman proud of her obvious secret.

'Blanka — '

'Oh, let's leave it alone. We said we weren't going to talk about that sort of thing any more.'

'You mean Veselka.'

'You don't suppose, do you,' she said owlishly, 'you don't suppose he's just sitting there letting himself be chopped up? Once things get back to normal — '

'What do you mean by normal?'

'If,' said Blanka. 'If, if, if. If they get back . . . if the old gang swing the pendulum, or' — she giggled — 'do whatever it

188

is you do with pendulums, then you know who'll be there to make it tick properly. You know who'll be ready with all the documentation they need on people to be arrested — intellectuals, kids, anyone who's spoken out of turn. The scapegoats'll be lined up, ready. Not the top people, of course — just a nice little assortment of middling folk, ready to be groomed for the show trials. You know who'll have *that* organised.' She reached for her glass and held it up very carefully, then took a long, slow drink from it. 'I expect you're back on the list now.'

'The list?'

'Since I left him,' said Blanka, 'I expect you've been put back on.' The last mouthful of wine seemed to have had an immediately depressant effect on her. 'Oh, God,' she said. Her lips drooped. 'Is this what you call giving your wife a good time? Is this the best you can do?'

When they got back to their hotel she opened her mouth for a long, wet kiss, and tugged at the hairs at the back of his neck, and leaned against him and closed her eyes.

He knew he had to say it. He said: 'Darling.'

Afterwards, with her head on his arm, their hips sticking lightly together where they touched, she seemed to doze for a while. Out of the dream she said lazily: 'Did you ever hear about Heydrich — the men who assassinated Heydrich during the war?'

'Too much. I was a boy then, and we lived only a few hundred yards off Resslova. They came stamping through the house, looking for the men who had done it.'

'When they'd caught them,' she whispered into the darkness. 'You know? Lidice, and the rest of it. And there was the woman who'd loved one of those men. When they got their hands on her, they showed her the man's head — pickled, in a bottle. Did you know that? The man she loved. The man she'd . . . she'd . . . '

She was clinging to him, rigid.

'Who told you this?' he said.

'Who do you think?'

'You've got to stop thinking about him.'

'He used to rave on about the Nazis and what they'd done,' she said. 'He wasn't much more than a child at the time, but he'd been told all about it. It got like a terrifying fairy-tale that he had to keep coming back to. And before you knew where you were, he was talking about our own people — men and women he'd had to deal with in his job — and what he could do with *them*. And then it was all right, when it was him doing it.' She shivered. It was impossible to tell whether the shiver was one of repugnance or of reawakened appetite. 'Do you know, sometimes he'd just sit there and cry. Cry!'

'It won't do you any good to go on about it.'

'Cry,' she repeated. 'Sitting there snivelling. And afterwards — '

'Blanka — '

'Afterwards he was worse than ever. It made him more . . . more vicious. More inventive.' Her whisper became a harsh, greedy croak. 'He wanted such awful things after he'd been crying.'

Her hand groped over his body; but

191

then, from one second to another, she had suddenly gone to sleep.

In the morning they went to see her aunt, who lived in a starchily respectable, dull street in Favoriten, a few minutes' walk from the Sud Bahnhof.

At first she refused to recognise Blanka. Then there were kisses and questions that still rang with peevishness, as though it had all been Blanka's fault that letters could not safely and honestly be sent from Prague to Vienna for so many years.

And then there were the questions about Jarmila. Jarmila, who had never shown up in Vienna. She hadn't come, and there had never been any word from her.

Blanka began to storm. Grudgingly her aunt put a call through to a remote relation in Munich, where it was just faintly possible Jarmila had gone.

No, they had heard nothing.

It was a sombre note. Blanka decided that it turned their second honeymoon to tragedy. 'The wicked old bitch,' she said when they had left Favoriten. 'She just doesn't want to be disturbed. She doesn't realise what it's been like for us, and she doesn't want to know.'

'Very few people do want to know,' Jan observed. 'It upsets them. They'd sooner not listen.'

'But Jarmila . . . when you think . . . '

She had probably been shot trying to cross the border. She had made an escape bid with two friends, and it was all too likely that they had been spotted, trapped in the wire, or shot down as they made a break for it. There was no way of finding out now. There had been too many such incidents. When your relations had run that obstacle course, you didn't check up whether they had fallen: you kept quiet, as you did about so many things.

'It's a good job you didn't go with her,' Jan said.

'Is it?' She turned on him as though he had spat at her. 'I wish you believed that. I wish I could be sure you believed that.'

★   ★   ★

The moment they got back to the flat, Jan felt that something was wrong. When he went on into the sitting-room he was sure. He nudged a drawer shut and prodded a small pile of books into another position.

'Do stop fussing.' Blanka had been getting more and more petulant as they approached home. 'You're like an old woman.'

'Has someone been in here while we've been away?'

He pointed to a mark on the linoleum where one leg of the bed had once stood. There was a corresponding mark close to the other leg, as though the bed had been shifted a few centimetres to one side.

'You're imagining things,' said Blanka.

He examined the heavy chest-of-drawers which had come to him from his father and mother. That stood where it had always stood, but there was a scar on the linoleum as though it might have been pulled out and pushed back.

'Perhaps when I was cleaning,' said Blanka.

Jan tried to move the chest, and couldn't budge it.

'You moved that?' he said.

'But who would want to come in and

push things like that about?'

He opened several drawers. He checked the titles in the bookcase to see if books had been moved. Even if only one had changed its place, he would have known. They were all in order. Yet he knew things had been moved: perhaps pulled out and then carefully replaced, but not carefully enough.

'Somebody's got you worried,' jeered Blanka. It was almost as though she was debating whether or not to change allegiance again.

He was tempted to ask whether the trip to Vienna had been a ruse — whether she had lured him out of the way while the flat was searched. But that was absurd. There were easier ways of doing it than that. It could have been thoroughly searched any day while Blanka was at the Radio and he was at the Institute — or even, if he had to contemplate the worst, while Blanka was present. She could perfectly well have searched it herself and found whatever they were looking for.

The map? But if it had been that and she had known about it, by now she would have let out some sly hint to tell him that she knew. She wouldn't have been able to restrain herself.

'*I* can't see anything missing,' said Blanka after a perfunctory look round the flat.

'No.'

'Then what on earth are you so edgy about?'

The mysterious sketch had travelled to and from Vienna, folded into the back of his wallet of road maps. If that was what they had searched the flat for, they had gone away empty-handed.

He still wanted to know why they had come for it at all. If they had come.

★ ★ ★

Jan was asked to serve on a committee for the rehabilitation of academics who had been persecuted for spurious political motives. All grievances were to be re-examined. Legal proceedings were to be instituted where appropriate.

Brok said how pleased he was, and Jan was tempted to refuse. Three or four younger members of the Institute, and

196

two older men from the University, implored him to accept. He was needed: he was known to be honest and unbiased.

'Is that how you see me?'

'Yes, Professor. Are you surprised?'

Refusal was out of the question.

He realised that the time had come, at last, when no honourable man could be private, wary, uncommitted. He flung himself into his work — the old work and the new — with renewed zest. The most pessimistic seer must surely respond to the propitious runes. The signs were favourable: it took unwavering application to keep the magic powerful.

Only believe.

Soon there would be another trip to England. And now there was no hurry, no impatience. They could all come and go as they pleased. Never again that fear, right up to the last minute, that some vindictive little functionary would decree that he could not leave.

The barriers were up and there was no need to fear: they were going to stay up.

8

The sun chased the shadow of the car along a bank and then sprawled it on the road ahead as Maggie slowed towards the barrier. She said something airy and meaningless to Jan, to demonstrate to the waiting frontier guards that he and she hadn't a care in the world.

There were two different uniforms on display. The Russians were easy to identify: grey-featured, sullen young men with tommy-guns slung across their chests.

A Czech came to the car and stooped beside Maggie's window. She produced her passport with its visa and currency slips tucked loosely inside. Jan leaned across with his documents.

Now, said Maggie to herself. Now. Any minute now.

One of the Russians shifted his weight from his right foot to his left.

The Czech spoke to Jan. Jan said in

English: 'He wants to inspect a case or two.'

'Oh, well.' Maggie began to open her door.

Jan said: 'I will do it. Stay where you are.'

He got out and unfastened the straps which lashed their baggage to the roof.

Maggie sat and stared at the bar across the road ahead. Fifty yards farther on was the Austrian hut. So close now.

When they had finished with the stuff off the roof, they'd get round to the interior of the car. And this plan here — what is it, please? Something military? The Russians a few paces forward, guns nosing in through the windows. Maybe they had a tank back there, ready to waddle out and crush her Renault just as Jan's Skoda had been crushed.

Then the guard began to strap the luggage back into place. He made a thorough job of it. Jan got back in. When the guard had finished he bent down once more. His face was set, but he closed his eye in one solemn wink, and jerked his head towards the Russians. He said something, and Jan translated:

'He says he had to show our Soviet brothers how thorough he is.'

They were waved on. The Russians stayed impassively where they stood. Maggie started slowly and tremulously, and stalled. The Czech guard indicated his willingness to give a shove. Maggie shook her head, and the car shot abruptly forward. They reached the Austrian checkpoint and were through in less than a minute.

Through. Free.

Maggie let out an explosive gasp. The world was suddenly wider, making her quite dizzy. The air was richer. The sun, on its way down, shone more brightly than it had done over those last dusty Bohemian miles.

She glanced at Jan. His head had sunk as though now, at last, knowing he was free, he was allowing himself to collapse. He looked despairing rather than relieved. Yet in that moment, when his face was drained — of life, colour, everything — she somehow saw through the stretched mask and saw Jan Melisek himself for the first time. There was a staunchness there that had nothing to do with the brusque or self-deprecating pedantry he had affected while they talked: a tenacity that would not be shaken, even by his own doubts of himself; a fine bone structure beneath the imperfect flesh.

Maggie drew the car in at the side of the road and switched off.

Jan raised his head. 'It has been a strain for you? You must need a rest.'

She kissed him.

She had already noticed that men in Prague smelt different. And now Jan tasted different from the Englishmen she had known — and from two Frenchmen, an American and one Italian she allowed herself to remember. Not just the staleness that she, too, must be breathing after their journey, but some immediate, vital difference.

'Thank you,' he said, absurdly grave and yet not absurd.

'The kiss of life,' said Maggie.

The colour had certainly come back into his cheeks. She felt it flooding into her own.

They set off again, and were in Linz by dusk.

Maggie found a parking place some yards from a hotel entrance. She changed her shoes, grabbed her bag from the back of the car and locked the doors.

Jan chuckled as they went into the hotel. She glanced inquiringly at him.

'If there is no room here?' he said.

'Then we try another.'

'So why do you bring your bag with you?'

Maggie swung the straw handle between her fingers. 'I told you, it's my grab-bag. It goes everywhere with me. I just grab it automatically.'

The desk clerk regretted that there were no rooms. At this time of year they were usually full, and now there were many people from Czechoslovakia here, staying or passing through. He offered the names of two other hotels, one of them only fifty yards along this same street. They left the car where it was, and walked along.

This time they were lucky. Two businessmen were giving up their rooms because friends escaping from Bratislava wished to meet them in Vienna.

'The rooms are not on the same floor,' the clerk said, faintly apologetic as he looked from Maggie to Jan and back again. His romantic soul was evidently perturbed by this inhospitable arrangement.

Jan filled in the registration pad without replying. Maggie followed suit.

There was a garage in converted stables at the back. They would have to drive to the end of the street, turn right down a one-way street, and turn right again and be sure not to miss the entrance, or another circuit would be obligatory.

They went to fetch the car.

It had gone.

Maggie stared at the empty space, disbelieving. She closed her eyes. Surely when she opened them the good, solid shape of the Renault would be there again?

But it had disappeared.

They went into the hotel which they had first tried. The clerk was distressed, but knew nothing about it. No, he did not think the police would have towed it away: that was not a common practice at this time of the evening.

The police confirmed that they had not towed the car away. They took details, but looked far from optimistic. There had been five such thefts already this last week.

It was too much. 'Too bloody much,' said Maggie aloud as they went back to their hotel. 'We get out . . . get this far . . . survive all that flap and all that dirty work at the crossroads — and now *this*!'

She had been looking forward to a long, soaky bath and a meal, an early night with clean pyjamas and a clean, comfortable bed.

'Now this,' she repeated.

'It is my fault,' said Jan. 'I'm sorry — you should have got rid of me sooner.'

'What?'

'It's me — or something I possess — which they are after.'

'Oh, it could happen to anyone. The police told us, five already in a week.'

'I think this is different. All my fault. If you hadn't stopped to give me a lift — '

'Oh, rubbish,' said Maggie. 'Anyway, it'll make a wonderful story when I get home.'

That was true. Even with this disaster upon them, she was already thinking of London as real, and the events of the last few days, even the last few hours, as being scenes in a rather lurid tale. She must make the most of it before the colours faded.

They would have to buy toothpaste, toothbrushes. Jan would find a barber's and have a shave in the morning.

And then . . . ? A hired car would be monstrously expensive. They would have to check train times, and work out some dreary sequence of journeys and changes across Europe. Or get plane bookings.

'But not now,' wailed Maggie. 'Not tonight. Let's clean up and go out and eat.'

'Yes. You'll be my guest.'

'It's on me. You'll need your English currency.'

'I insist.'

'Oh, go and get washed,' said Maggie. And then, as they were about to part, she said: 'If it *is* that sinister sketch of yours they're after, they're going to be disappointed, aren't they?'

'Please?'

She swung her grab-bag to and fro so that it creaked. 'It's in here,' she said. 'Still safe. For what it's worth.'

'For what it's worth,' he mused. He shrugged his incomprehension. 'Yes.'

* * *

At dinner, to an ebbing and flowing ripple of violin and accordion music, she tried to cheer him up. He was tired, and gloomy over what he considered his responsibility for the theft of her car. Maggie, doggedly and deliberately inconsequential, refused to deal with this topic.

'What will you do when you get to England?' she asked.

'I hope to lecture, if they will let me. And write, and perhaps translate. First of all I will see my publisher — throw myself on his mercy.'

'And sell him a thriller about your creepy map?'

'The map . . .'

Gradually he thawed. Trying to work out what the map could possibly be, he had to tell her a lot about the background; and once he had started, his slowly, steadily burning enthusiasm for his subject illuminated the evening.

It was an odd theme for a dinner-table conversation between two strangers, thrown together as disconcertingly as they had been. Yet he made it live. The candles on the table flickered and burned down, but Maggie was not conscious of time passing.

For him, archaeology was no dead subject. He sketched in parallels which had already been intimated during their drive past the harvest fields — the all-too-familiar patterns of civilisations which had destroyed themselves, communities which had cracked up from within because of vanity and jealousy, communities which had developed both social order and craftsmanship to a high pitch and then been debased or shattered by waves of barbarism. Struggles upwards, then crumbling despair. The cultural rise of Celtic skills in iron and pottery, their growing sophistication; and then defeat and dispersal as they were crushed between the Roman Empire pressing in from the south and the Teutons trampling in from the north.

Many Celtic treasures were saved, removed, and to all appearances offered up to the gods. Some had been found strangely buried in the peat bogs of Denmark. The bronze cauldron at Braa, the great silver bowl of Gundestrup: had these rich, exquisite objects been interred in a last, despairing religious sacrifice?

'That map of yours,' hazarded Maggie: 'was that to do with buried treasures, or with people?'

'My friend must have sketched it in a great hurry, perhaps as no more than an *aide-memoire*. It could have been either representational objects or bodies.'

'You said it couldn't be a burial ground.'

'Oh no. It *could* be. But if it is, it's unique. In Sumava there are many Celtic oppida, but always one thing is lacking. There are the settlements, and very substantial ones, commanding the valleys — well fortified, highly civilised. But no cemeteries.'

The candle flames swayed. The waiter hovered, keeping an eye on the wine bottle.

'Cemeteries?' It was incongruous. Maggie had to laugh. 'That's something to perplex you?'

'Yes. In this late La Tene period, with every indication of a highly sophisticated civilisation, there are no burial grounds. Nothing. Neither the skeleton graves nor the cremation grounds of the earlier period. What did they do with their dead?'

'Well . . . fashions change,' Maggie offered feebly.

'Yes. We would like to know how they changed, and in what direction. The ritual conventions must have altered. But we've never had any indication . . . never found a trace . . . '

'Until your friend produced that scribble?'

'It doesn't belong,' said Jan with an anguish which was beyond her. She supposed he must lie awake and worry about this sort of thing night after night, the way she very occasionally fretted over a face or name she half remembered, or the title of a film that eluded her. 'The map' — he half closed his eyes, and she realised that the lines of the sketch were so indelibly etched on his mind that he might as well throw the sheet of paper away — 'shows a group of shapes which might be bodies. Near both Zdikov and Zdikovec there are peat bogs. The Tollund man in Jutland lay well preserved in such a bog for two thousand years after a ritual strangling. It may be that Lada, searching for Slavonic remains, found a cache to interest me instead.'

'Something weird enough to get him rubbed out?'

'I keep saying to myself that what happened to him can have had nothing to do with the map. He must have been involved in some other unsavoury mess. And yet, why did he cram it into my letter-box like that?'

'It couldn't have something to do with a secret code? You read so much about these microdots and . . . well . . . '

'Invisible ink?' He smiled. 'I must admit I've held it up to the light, but I don't have the apparatus for more intensive examination.'

'And you never tried to track down the actual site?'

'Oh yes. Yes, I tried.'

'And?'

'I was interrupted.'

He began to tell her about it. She was struck by his detachment. The leap across the frontier had affected him rather as it had affected her: emotion recollected in tranquillity, climactic scenes from remote melodrama summed up in matter-of-fact phrases.

'My wife was invited to spend a few days with her married cousin in Nymburk. Cousin Olga knew we'd been to Vienna, and wanted to hear about it, and about Jarmila. Blanka, naturally . . . '

Blanka, naturally, wanted to show off. She wanted to talk knowledgeably about Vienna and to hint at future travels further afield. Also she was not reluctant to hint darkly at Jarmila's probable fate.

Cousin Olga had been quaking for years, ever since Jarmila left. She was a sister, they were bound to pick on her and penalise her. On more than one occasion Blanka had cattily attributed Olga's hasty marriage to her fears about the runaway. Only the change of name could have tempted her. With a bit of luck, snoopers wouldn't connect her with the girl who had defected. She married, and she and her husband lived unhappily ever after.

It was almost time for the trip to England which Jan had promised. They applied for visas. They would leave only a few days after Blanka got back from Nymburk.

She said: 'While I'm away — '

'While you're away,' he said, 'I think I'll go down to Sumava.'

'Whatever for?'

'To follow up a lead. Something interesting.'

'What kind of lead?'

They were in the sitting-room. Blanka walked to and fro, picking up things she thought she might need, then discarding half of them. Jan said:

'Something Ladislav Adamec put me on to, quite a time ago.'

'Before he died?'

'As it happens, before he died.'

'There's no need to be sarcastic.'

'Well, he could hardly have given it to me . . .'

Jan stopped. Because, of course, it had come to him in fact after Ladislav had died.

Blanka had stopped fussing from drawer to suitcase. She stood with one elbow on the chest-of-drawers and said: 'Jan, there wasn't . . . wasn't something special, was there? Something Adamec gave you?'

'What would he have given me?'

'I don't know. I'm asking you.'

'I've told you. An interesting lead. And what makes you ask, anyway?'

'Just that with all that trouble . . . that terrible business . . . oh, never mind.'

Blanka applied herself to her packing. It was on the tip of his tongue to mention the map outright and see what he could jolt out of her, but at the last second he decided not to.

When he had seen her off from the station he drove southwards, choosing to stay first at Zdikov. He would try his luck there, then move on if he had time.

He found a small country hospoda a mile outside the village, set in dark pines above a stream.

'Even in summer,' he reminisced to Maggie, 'it's quiet there. There aren't all that many villages in the borderland — it's proved too risky to live there in the past, with armies always wanting to storm over you. Granite peaks, forests, wild game . . . somehow it is raw and at the same time soothing and beautiful. There are paper-mills, but they are hidden in the forests. Some glassworks. And campers and holidaymakers — yet even at the height of the season, a sense of peace. It slows one down. Makes it difficult to work, if you are foolish enough to go there to work.'

A man and his wife ran the hospoda with the aid of one surly but conscientious elderly woman. They were used to stray visitors, campers who had wearied of camping, and the occasional teacher or works manager seeking a few days of primitive life which would not be too devastatingly primitive. They liked to talk, but for years must have bottled it up. Today everybody, everywhere, was talking — talking freely at last. In the evenings two burly men from a local sawmill would settle at a corner table and start drinking. They were joined in due course by a thinner, nervy middle-aged man who wore a clamantly turquoise pen and a ballpoint clipped in his breast pocket. When things were not too busy the landlord sat with them, while his wife dodged to and fro, contributing disjointed remarks like someone determined to wreck a poker game.

Mr and Mrs Rakovec had a son. The mention of his name signalled an argument which showed all the signs of being a new experience for them. They had kept quiet for a long time. Now they could make up for it.

The boy had gone off hurriedly to Prague, years ago. There had been no word from him. It was a common enough thing in this part of the country — kids wanting the bright lights, finding nothing to do here, packing up and leaving . . . 'No time for us any more.' But at least they ought to write.

A woman with her husband at an adjoining table said that their son and daughter came home regularly, and wrote every week without fail.

The man with the pens hinted that the Rakovec boy had got himself into trouble. 'Or maybe it was a girl he got into trouble,' he winked at Rakovec.

Mrs Rakovec, passing, flared up. 'He was a good boy, my Josef. He had to go away because the secret police were here, on the prowl — and *that's* no disgrace to him, is it? He was helping people to escape over the hills into Bavaria. When things were bad, *he* had the courage. Not like some.'

'Maybe he helped once too often, and they — '

'No!' cried the mother.

'They took him away,' the man finished lamely.

'He's in Prague,' she insisted. 'He had to run for it, but he's safe. We'd have heard if anything had happened.'

'And if nothing happened, why didn't you hear, then? If he was such a good boy — '

'He won't bring trouble on us by getting in touch, that's why.'

It was all sadly familiar to Jan. He thought of Blanka's cousin, and of the speculations and laments which Blanka and Olga were probably exchanging right at this moment. Perhaps Jarmila did get away, after all. Perhaps the Rakovec boy was in Prague, being over-cautious. Or perhaps — and didn't the mother ever allow herself to think this? — he was nothing now but a fertilising pulp in some field just this side, or just the other side, of the frontier wire.

'But things are better now,' the man with the pens was saying. 'I can vouch for that. In my work, it shows very soon — you soon know which way the wind's blowing. No reason why Josef shouldn't come back and see you now, if he wanted to.'

'You never did like him, did you?' spat Mrs Rakovec.

One of the men from the sawmill drank his beer down and looked appreciatively at the fluffy froth clinging to the glass. 'My lad works in the brewery at Plzen. Sends money home. Goes to see his mother regularly.'

'More regularly than you do,' growled his friend.

The usual provincial bickerings, the feuds without vindictiveness, the slow pulse of a small community: even in argument it was seductive, sapping the will to do anything but sit and drink, talk, listen, drowse.

Jan forced himself to concentrate on his quest.

He struck out 5 kilometres to the south-east of the village. Or was that 5 an 8?

He found himself on the side of a valley, looking down on a confluence of brooks. None of his researches had ever indicated that there were Celtic settlements in this immediate area; but there was a record of some so far unidentified configurations on the slope of the farther valley.

He could walk over that way, or explore down this one, looking for something that would trigger off a response in his mind.

In the end he decided to stay in this valley. By late afternoon he had walked a long way and found nothing. He returned to the hospoda, not unduly disappointed. In this profession you spent most of your time trudging along false trails, torn between deduction and guesswork which ought to be inspired but often wasn't.

Next day he studied his maps. Already he was wavering, wondering whether he should have plumped for Zdikovec. If the scribble and the wobbly figure operated from there, it would not be too difficult to take the car across country from the hospoda and intersect the line. The lanes would be bumpy, but he could find somewhere over there to park and then start walking again.

He set out.

It was not until late in the day, scrambling through the woods and down the sides of valleys, that he came upon the peat bog. The nearer side was soft and spongey, giving off a faint sulphurous smell and plopping up little bubbles along the rim. The far side of the valley looked firmer.

'A peat bog!' said Maggie as he told her. 'Like the Danish burial grounds, where there was all that treasure and stuff?'

'It did seem promising. The bog wasn't a likely place for a settlement, of course, but the hill above could have provided the basis for a fortification. It would bear investigation. The next day I planned to drive round the far side of the valley and start from there.'

'And . . . ?'

That evening he had lazed contentedly in the smoky atmosphere of the hospoda. Mrs Rakovec had tried to talk optimistically about her Josef; the man with the pens made a few asides which seemed to hint that he had many reservations about the Rakovec boy; the two from the sawmill discussed a new works committee which was going to have a say in the management not only of the works but of future political nominations; and Mr Rakovec said it would all be the same in the end, there would be no real reforms, it was all a lot of talk.

'Just like an English pub!' Jan said to Maggie. 'It was blissful, for those few hours. At last!'

'And,' she prompted him again, 'next day?'

'Next day,' he said, 'the Russians and their pals were over our frontiers.'

When he came down in the morning, the landlord and his wife were sitting numbly beside the radio. No breakfast had been prepared. Voices ranted on.

Russians, Hungarians, Poles, Bulgarians: which would take up positions here, which would arrive first? Surely they wouldn't risk a direct confrontation of East Germans with West Germans?

Perhaps they were already here — already out there in the woods, ringing the towns and villages, preparing for whatever it was they had decided to do.

Jan tried to phone Blanka. Lines were in chaos. The invaders had already occupied the Prague telephone exchange.

'So I started back at once, to Prague,' said Jan.

'And now we'll never know,' said Maggie. 'About that map, I mean.'

'No, I suppose not.'

* * *

When they said good night he kissed her. His hands rested on her shoulders for a long time, and she thought he was going to say something and she had no idea what her answer would be. Then he kissed her again, quickly and affectionately, and let her go; and she didn't have to make a decision.

She slept naked because there was nothing else to do. Jan Melisek, in another room on another floor, would be the same. She lay on her back with her hands folded across her belly and thought about him. Then she tried not to think about him.

'Maggie Armitage,' she said aloud, reprovingly.

Maggie Armitage seemed in no mood to listen. She thought that there was nothing to stop him coming to her room and coming in. Nothing except herself.

And would she stop him?

But he wouldn't come. She knew that. And it was just as well, because really it would be just a bit much, first day they'd met, first night . . .

She wasn't ready for that sort of thing. Not yet.

'Stop it,' she exhorted herself. 'Think beautiful thoughts.'

She thought about Jan. And really, the thoughts were quite beautiful.

Maggie turned on her side and tried to think of something else. Arnold, for example. She conjured up a picture of him, and at once started contrasting him with Jan. That was unfair; and it certainly didn't help her to go off to sleep. So she substituted a picture of Mrs Chinnery, and that did the trick: by blurred stages she sank into an interminable dream about Mrs Chinnery.

At breakfast the next morning there was a phone call to their hotel from the hotel along the road. The car had been returned intact and was back at its place by the kerb.

'It is because they find Czech luggage,'

the manager explained. 'There was an incident just like this in Vienna the other day. I hear of one in Italy, also. People are sympathetic. Even thieves, they have feelings. There is much goodwill.' He spoke as though it were a special service provided by the management.

Jan was dubious. He still believed that someone had been tipped off from across the border — someone had been after the map.

'Then why bother to return the car?' Maggie demanded logically.

He had no answer.

They drove off in good spirits. It could have been a holiday, a tourist jaunt across Europe, taking in Salzburg, Munich, Strasbourg, all the way to the French frontier along the autobahn.

They spent a night in an ageing but adequate hotel outside Nancy. Maggie didn't wonder whether Jan would make any passes at her this time. She knew he wouldn't. But she found, to her great irritation, that she was lying awake wondering what would happen when they reached England — when he was free, when there were no obligations on him, when they were individuals and he could choose whether to go on seeing her or not.

Free? She still didn't know the full story about his wife. Where was the shadowy Blanka, of whom she knew so little?

Before, she might have asked some more direct questions. Now, for some reason, it was impossible. There had been a subtle shift in their relationship. Or was this just something she imagined because she wanted it to be that way?

They drove on, and reached Calais in time to see a ferry heading out into the Channel. At least this meant they were first in line for the next boat. They found the ticket office, drove to the quay and waited in a huge shed like a job-lot aeroplane hangar.

It was all too simple now. There was a quick passport inspection; no Customs check. When the ferry was ready, she drove on board and they went up to the Immigration Officer's little cabin.

'You intend to stay long in England, Professor?'

'I wish to seek asylum.'

'Ah, yes. Please consult my senior officer at the other end. I'm sure there won't be any snags.' His smile was a trifle stiff, but sincere. 'I hope things go well for you, sir.'

The crossing took ninety minutes. A party of school children ran up and down, along the deck, down a companionway, their voices echoing hollowly away and then returning with renewed vigour. Jan looked back at the creamy wake. He began to look lost and remote again; not believing, not sure of anything.

At Dover he was issued with a visitor's visa for a month, and politely told that he must apply to the Home Office for an extension.

Maggie drove the car off.

'As easy as that!' she said encouragingly.

He nodded, speechless.

Before they could reach the Customs, two men stepped forward, peering at Maggie's car as though to make sure of identification, and then flagging her down.

'Professor Melisek?'

Jan stiffened. No, said Maggie silently: not now, not trouble now, after we've got this far.

'Would you mind accompanying us, sir?'

Jan looked at her. Maggie put her hand over his and squeezed it.

'Some piddling little formality,' she said.

'Yes, of course.'

He got out. Maggie drew the car to one side to let others pass.

By the end of ten minutes she had bitten a ragged arc out of her right thumb-nail. She wanted them to be on their way, up the road to London. They would discuss where he was going to stay and what she could do to help and where and when they would meet . . .

A porter came towards the car, with a more smartly uniformed Customs officer a few paces behind.

'Which are Mr Mellyshick's bags, miss?'

'What's happened?'

'It's just that his gear's wanted off, that's all.'

'But how long's he going to be?'

'You're not to wait, miss. The gentleman's grateful for what you've done for him, and says not to worry. He'll be in touch when he can. But he doesn't want you to hang around here for ages.'

'Why does it have to be ages?'

'The bags — if you'd just tell us which ones . . . '

The cases were unstrapped. The porter put them neatly to one side and looked vaguely into the car.

'That the lot, miss?'

Maggie knew, shatteringly, that something was dead wrong and she might not see Jan Melisek again. None of it was really anything to do with her. None of it. Not even the map that was still tucked into her grab-bag: the map that made no sense, any more than the accompanying violence made sense.

Stonily she said: 'Yes, that's the lot.'

228

9

There were two of them. One wore a tie which Jan classified as proclaiming loyalty to a school, a college, a regiment or a golf club. His smattering of British mythology was too meagre to tell him which. In spite of their quiet courtesy, he was sure the two men intended to discredit whatever he might say. They were listening for a false note which would somehow give him away.

Yet they were not threatening. He was in England. Only just here, just over the edge; but in England. They were glacial and mistrustful but they had their rules: they were no kin to the thugs he had left behind him.

'Now, Professor . . . '

'May I be told who I am talking to?'

The men exchanged glances. Then the shorter of the two said pleasantly: 'My name's Gould.'

'And mine's Jones.'

Jan laughed.

'Really it is.' Gould shared the laugh, but his eyes stayed chill and dispassionate. 'My friend Jones is none other than my friend Jones.' He tolerated a moment's delay, then repeated: 'Now, Professor . . .'

It sounded friendly, as though they were contemplating helping him. But they weren't giving: they wanted something from him.

'What am I here for?' asked Jan.

'We were hoping you would tell us that.'

'I was brought to this office — '

'In this country,' said Gould. 'Why have you come to England?'

'I'd have thought it was obvious. I am . . .' Until now he had not thought of the word in all its starkness. 'I'm a refugee.'

Gould nodded. 'You have a valid passport. Visa. All in order. All prepared — *before* the invasion.'

'That was because we were planning — '

'Do you intend to go back, or to stay?'

'I am seeking political asylum.'

Again Gould nodded, and Jones aped him.

It was Jones who said: 'Do you object to your luggage being searched?'

'Not at all.'

'And if it should prove necessary' — Jones smiled as Veselka might have smiled, making a man-to-man joke of it, yet with the cautious deference of a genuine request rather than intimidation — 'we may search you personally?'

'If you must.'

Gould's right forefinger tapped the table. 'I wonder if you'd mind emptying your pockets.'

Jan tipped out his diary, his wallet, a bunch of keys, and a few tickets and scraps of paper he had accumulated. He felt ashamed of his crumpled, grimy handkerchief.

Jones began to pick over the items on the table.

Gould said: 'Will you tell us why you decided to leave your country, Professor — and why you chose to come to England?'

It all seemed so plain and self-evident to Jan that he didn't know where to start. But Gould, like a skilled television interviewer, nudged him gently this way and that, and laid down the guide-lines. Unlike a television programme, there was no appointed end. Time meant nothing. They would steer him patiently until he was finally headed the way they wanted him to go.

He felt that he had told the story so often. Part of it to Maggie Armitage in a jumbled sort of way, and heaven knew how many times to himself, sifting it and then processing it again, shovelling and sifting until it had all gone dry and stale and unconvincing. Now, facing these two inquisitors, he couldn't summon up the energy to provide more than a digest version. There had been a time — more than one occasion — when he had wanted desperately to talk to someone, to talk it all out obsessively and try to establish some reasoning behind it all; but now *they* wanted him to talk, and that wasn't the same thing at all.

Not too much about Blanka. Nothing too personal, too revealing. He felt the prod of a question, and evaded it. And he skirted round the business of the map, because how could he tell them anything which would do him any good, when he didn't know its significance anyway?

'But you refused to co-operate with this S.T.B. executive?'

The word 'executive' came out with a certain respect, as though it were no shameful thing to be on that level. Perhaps to them it was in fact an acknowledgment of quasi-military rank: an enemy captain was still a captain, entitled to a salute.

'There's no reason for me to lie to you,' said Jan. 'No reason why I shouldn't be telling the truth.'

'None at all.'

Gould gave the impression of not caring much whether he heard the truth or not. All he wanted was something which would fit in with his own tangled thinking: something to use against someone in a given set of circumstances — perhaps, wanton and aimless, against Jan himself.

At one stage Jan, lulled by the lack of any hectoring stridency in the interrogation, found that he had allowed an implication to build up that he had drifted along with Veselka on a few minor matters.

'But this is ridiculous,' he burst out. 'What was there to spy on? Who would I have spied on? I've told you, I wasn't the type: I have never had anything to do with that sort of infantile snakes and ladders.'

Not the most tactful thing to say, in view of the obvious devotion of these two men to their duty.

Jones turned over a slip of paper and studied it. He passed it to Gould, who pursed his lips and abruptly asked: 'Professor Melisek, we have been instructed, and our Embassy in Prague has been instructed, that every facility is to be offered to anyone whose life or liberty may be imperilled by the Soviet invasion. Nobody in real danger is to be turned away.'

'It is what I expected. Always, when I think of your country — '

'What made you think of it so conveniently in advance?'

Jan did not grasp this. Then he recalled the earlier sly inference. 'My wife and I had already arranged our visas for a holiday in England.'

'Together?'

'Yes.'

'But she is not with you now. She didn't come?'

'There were . . . reasons.'

'You would like to state them?'

Jan was silent. They wanted too much. Official inquiries, yes. Security measures, very well: this was reasonable. But to scratch down into the shrinking truth inside him, about personal pains which could not possibly concern them . . .

'Did *they* insist,' asked Gould blandly, 'that you leave her at home as a guarantee of good conduct?'

'You have it wrong. Quite wrong.'

'Professor, we don't wish to distress you. Simple answers to simple questions will help us to settle things one way or the other. As I've said, anyone with good reason to believe himself in danger from the Russians or any of their collaborators is welcome in this country. Tell me: why did you feel personally threatened?'

'After my refusal to co-operate with the S.T.B. — '

'You did refuse?'

'I've told you so.'

'Ah, yes. Yes, you did tell us.'

'I was marked down. They were ready to take me in when the word was given. Those few days before I left — '

'Tell us about them, Professor. What was so alarming about those few days — alarming to you personally, bad enough to make you leave your wife, your work, everything . . . and make a dash for it?'

★　★　★

He had taken a wary, weaving route back to Prague, on the alert for Russian tanks or troop movements. At one point he came full upon an armoured column and had no chance of dodging. He drove straight on, hugging the verge, and there was no attempt to halt him.

In Prague the only vehicles in sight were tanks, tanks, tanks: few of them moving, most of them lowering round street corners, blocking the way.

Indoors, he felt giddy. He sat down and

waited for his heart to stop pounding, then tried to ring Blanka. It was still impossible to get through.

The street outside was unnaturally quiet. It was a simmering stillness. You waited for the lid to blow off.

He switched on the radio.

Rumours, exhortations. 'Stay calm . . . act normally.'

Was that normal — deserted streets, shuttered shops, tanks on the corners and in the square by the tram-stop?

He wondered whether he ought to get out of the flat and stay out. The secret police would be emerging from their warrens again. Perhaps handing over names to the Russians, and organising deaths and disappearances.

But it was still unreal. He stayed in, numbed. At night there was a complete blackout. Throughout the hours of suffocating darkness there were sporadic stutters of gunfire, sometimes an isolated shot. Probably an apprehensive Ivan potting at shadows.

In the morning Jan joined a long queue for bread, and went on to another queue for tinned food. In the middle of the morning he walked down into the city.

A Czech Army truck rattled past with the word SVOBODA daubed on it. Two young men were hanging a banner from a high window, and there were placards stuck to trees and lamp-posts. *Russians go home . . . Moscow first right, second left . . .*

Jan went to the Institute.

A Russian soldier on duty at the door barred the way and asked a question in Russian. Jan spoke Czech back at him. Behind the guard, Brok appeared unexpectedly and stared at Jan.

'What are you doing here?'

'I wanted to see how things were.'

'And now you see. I *knew*. I knew,' said Brok, 'that things were going too fast. It was a terrible mistake. I said so all along.'

From somewhere inside the building came the lonely rattle of a single typewriter.

'Go home,' said Brok nervously. 'Go home and stay there. No point in coming in here. Not yet. Not for a while.'

Jan went home and tried again to

phone Blanka, with the same lack of success.

He went out to join another food queue. A face caught his attention: the face of a sallow young man leaning with his hands in his pockets against a house opposite.

In a district like this you knew when a stranger showed up, particularly when he showed up more frequently than was reasonable. That same face had been watching the bread queue this morning.

He was being followed. Ludicrous that in the present turmoil he should have been selected. Surely there were more dangerous antagonists? But then, he wouldn't be the only one: there must be scores of others, all being watched until somewhere a decision was confirmed and they were all rounded up.

Blanka telephoned late on Friday afternoon.

Was he all right? She wanted to get home. There was a bus coming into Prague tomorrow, due to arrive at about five o'clock. Could he meet her at the terminal? 'Please, Jan, please meet me. I couldn't bear to walk through those streets on my own. You'll meet me, won't you?'

He promised that he would.

'I'll try to ring just before I leave, when I know the bus is definitely running.'

On Saturday he heard a few trams grinding along in the morning. At noon there was news that talks were starting in Moscow and that both Dubcek and Cernik were present. It couldn't be more than a rumour — couldn't be.

Yet the announcer's voice tingled with hope. Jan allowed himself a moment of hope, too.

Then he looked out of the window. A man was staring into the window of the tobacconist's across the street. If not the same man, then one of the same type.

Early in the afternoon Blanka telephoned to say that the bus would be running and that she would be on it.

He allowed himself plenty of time when he set off to meet her, in case he had to walk the whole way.

There were four people waiting at the tram-stop. He decided to join them and see what came along. A minute later another man crossed the road and stood on the far end of the shallow island.

A tram came grinding up the hill. Jan waited until the last moment, then sprang on. The man at the end of the island came to life and also jumped for the platform.

Jan stood by the door. The man tipped his grey hat forward an inch or two and slumped into a corner seat. When the conductress came along, he asked where he had to change for Krizovnicka. 'Spejchar,' she muttered, and gave him a ticket.

Jan had only one stop to travel before getting off at the interchange point. If the man in the grey hat really wanted Krizovnicka, he ought to stay on until the stop beyond that. But when Jan got off, he got off.

There was plenty of time. Jan determined to put the man to the test and satisfy himself whether or not he was really being trailed.

The trams were running to no sort of timetable. A Number 8 came along, then there was a delay, and then a Number 1 closely followed by a 20. Jan let them go. The man let them go.

Finally, when every possible number had gone past, Jan abruptly chose a Number 1. He expected his shadow to flit up the steps as well. Instead, the man stayed behind. Looking back, Jan saw him cross the road — looking for a telephone box?

There was a crowd at the terminal. A bus came in and emptied, and there was a chattering reunion between children and waiting parents. Within five minutes the crowd had thinned and there were only half a dozen people left. One was a thin man who appeared to be reading a time-table. There wasn't much point in that, in the present circumstances.

They can't have watchers all over the city just waiting for me to show up, thought Jan. Not at a time like this.

Who do they think I could possibly be meeting — a correspondent from the *New York Times*?

Blanka's bus was late.

More people arrived, waiting perhaps

for that or perhaps for another bus. On impulse, Jan mingled with them and then hurried across the road. A bright yellow mechanical shovel, daubed with clay and mud, was tilted above a hole where tramlines were being repaired. Jan dodged behind it. Through the slumped arms of the shovel he saw the thin man fighting his way clear of the crowd and looked desperately around.

A younger man appeared suddenly and sauntered round the shovel. He saw Jan and continued his circuit. As he turned back towards the bus station he wiped his left hand slowly down the side of his head.

The other man relaxed.

The bus came in at last. Children and a few adults got off. Blanka was not among them.

Jan stayed for another hour in case there was a relief bus. It was odd that Blanka had phoned to say everything was all right, and now had somehow failed to get here.

While he hung about, the two men also hung about.

If they wanted to frame him, why stay here? If they were at all competent at their job they must know he was innocent of any offence: so if there was any accusation they wanted to make, obviously it had to be a put-up job. If they were watching him so assiduously now, it could only be a matter of keeping an eye on him until they were ready.

And yet, the purposeless waiting at this bus terminal . . .

Something that was not, as yet, even a suspicion began to itch at the back of his mind. He had been watched all the way from home, yes? Yes. They couldn't be suspecting him of anything because they knew there was nothing of which he was guilty. They couldn't catch him out in treachery because he wasn't involved in anything treacherous. All they were doing was making sure he stayed where he was. Why?

Blanka had not arrived on the bus, though she had telephoned to say she would certainly be on it.

If . . .

An absurd 'if'. But now, with Veselka

rising once more into the ascendant . . .

No, it was unthinkable.

He hurried home.

As soon as he opened the door into the flat he knew that Blanka had been here. She had been, and now she had gone. He opened the door of the deep cupboard which they had converted into a wardrobe. Blanka's clothes had been removed. He explored the flat and found none of her personal belongings left. She had been allowed plenty of time to do her packing.

The phone rang. It was Blanka.

Jan said: 'Your movement control reports are right on the dot, aren't they?'

'Jan, I'd have left a note, but I thought it was safer not to. Safer for both of us.'

He laughed. A note would have been so much politer!

'You think it's funny?' she said.

'Not very. You fix a game of hide and seek to keep me occupied while you sneak off. You've always loved rows, but you haven't the guts to face me when it's an important one. No, not very funny. What's got into you? Changing sides like a camp-follower. Do you think you'll get away with it? Do you think — '

'Jan, I'm sorry. But I'm sure this is best — '

'For both of us,' he finished for her.

'I wish you could understand.'

'I'm very understanding. I understand you're scared stiff — and that you're a cheat and a pervert.'

There was a pause. Then Blanka said, with a throbbing soulfulness which filled the room as it had so often filled it before: 'Jan, what will you do?'

'Your boss wants a report on my future programme?'

'Jan, please.'

'Tell him I don't hand out free information. His bloodhounds will have to work for their meat.'

'Jan, I must go.' Then she said: 'You *will* be all right, won't you?' Before he could think of a suitable reply she had rung off.

He poured himself a drink and sat down. Whatever happened now, he was well and truly on his own.

Perhaps nothing would happen. The whole grim comedy had apparently been personal rather than political. Veselka, still infatuated, had been biding his time and had now reclaimed Blanka. His watchers had ensured that her husband stayed out of the way while she got clear, and now maybe would be called off.

He thought idly of going to the Radio and having a showdown with Blanka. But she wouldn't be there. The Russians were running the place. Only the clandestine radio was the true voice of Prague now.

He went to bed early. At two in the morning he came suddenly wide awake. In his mind there exploded the memory of how the furniture had been moved while he and Blanka were in Vienna.

Jan got out of bed, made sure the curtains were tightly drawn, and switched on the light. He put his shoulder against the ponderous chest-of-drawers and heaved until it squawked across the floor.

Jutting from the linoleum behind it was what looked like a squat brass bolt. Jan touched it gingerly, then got a grip, rocked it to and fro, and in a blazing rage managed to wrench it clear.

He examined the object. A strand of

broken wire dangled from the underside.

He didn't know whether it was simply a microphone, with a lead that trailed away somewhere under the floor, or whether it was a transmitter.

Was this why Blanka had gone away with him to Vienna?

But that was unnecessary. If she had known about the bug, she could have let them instal it at any time.

She *must* have known it was there. And had she acted as an agent provocateur, drawing him on to say things Veselka wanted him to say, coaxing him into recording things on tape that could be edited into self-condemning form? But what things?

He made a pot of coffee, sat down and forced himself to think back.

He hadn't said anything treasonable to Blanka — anything that could be used against him. Had he? How on earth can you remember every remark you've made, everything you've casually said over days and weeks?

Think. Assume that an interrogator will be in a position to quote your own words back at you, selecting what he wants from your conversation and shuffling it into a feasible pattern. What do you wish you hadn't said? What can be twisted, snatched out of context, damningly reshaped?

He thought of the English money he still had. Blanka knew about that, certainly. She didn't know how much he held, but knew he had some. Perhaps they had mentioned it while discussing their English holiday.

Had he told her the joke about the economic plan and the Bohemian Knights under Blanik? Or that one about the schoolboy who had recited a list of adjacent friendly countries but had omitted our Russian brothers — 'Because you can choose your friends but you can't choose your brothers'?

Did I say, long ago, that Novotny was mentally defective, and the Soviet Union was Tsarist-Imperialist? *How* long ago?

Unless you're a deaf mute or a Trappist by choice, how can life be either tolerable or safe?

His grandfather's pistol . . .

Surely it was only a week or two back that he had made a facetious remark about the gun to Blanka: made it not far from that unsleeping little creature in the floor.

He wondered if the wire went down through the ceiling into the flat below. The man — he knew him only slightly — was a minor official in the Foreign Office. Was it part of his job to monitor messages from the flat above, to change tapes on a recorder . . . ?

A cache of Western arms. All part of the plot for an uprising, for the overthrow of socialist democracy in Czechoslovakia.

Who would believe such grotesque nonsense?

It was no more grotesque than the lies being spewed out by the Russian-sponsored Radio Vltava.

The pistol had belonged to his mother's father and was a relic of the First World War. It had been passed to Jan with his mother's few remaining effects when she died, and had been on the shallow top shelf of the cupboard ever since. It was coated with dust and there was no ammunition. But anyone who wanted to declare that it was a cache of British firearms could declare it was a cache of British firearms.

He went to the cupboard. The gun was there, pushed back behind his scarf and an old pullover.

When dawn had established itself and he could be reasonably confident that no nervy Russian youngster would squeeze a trigger at the mere sight of him, he went down to their cellar lock-up and found two bucketfuls of old potatoes left over from the winter. He wrapped the pistol in paper and thrust it deep into one of the buckets. Then he went out into the silent street, where two tall dustbins stood as usual on either side of the entrance. He lifted the lid of one and tipped a bucketful of musty potatoes in.

There was nobody in the street. He lifted the second bucket and began to tilt it. The paper round the gun rustled, and as a few potatoes spilled over into the bin he saw the padded shape emerge.

He stopped, and looked both ways along the pavement. It was insanely reckless that he should be tipping an incriminating weapon into a dustbin on his own doorstep.

He retrieved the package and slid it under his jacket, and took the buckets back indoors. Then he strolled out again and went as casually as possible along the street to the square. A tank squatted on the far side. A woman, her pinched face testifying to a sleepless night, pushed a pram with a squalling baby under the Russian gun as though nothing could get any worse.

Jan walked for ten minutes until he reached a long street with its own array of dustbins. The lid of one was perched rakishly to one side. He made sure nobody was watching, then poked the pistol and its wrappings through the gap. It fell with a clatter. He walked quickly on and went home by a different route.

Near the front door to the flats he saw a bruised potato and a few shreds of brown skin lying on the pavement. He was sure he had spilt none.

He could hardly stop and investigate. He went indoors, forced himself to wait five minutes, and then took down a pailful of authentic rubbish. When he lifted the lid, he found the bin empty save for a few slimy fragments at the bottom. All the potatoes he had dumped there not so long ago had been removed.

Jan went back upstairs.

They wouldn't find the gun — unless they had tracked him every inch of the way.

But what could they prove, even then?

Remembering the nineteen-fifties, remembering the whispers that had faded, the voices you no longer heard and didn't ask about, he knew that they didn't have to prove anything. Once they got started, they did what they had all along intended to do. It was really a waste of time for them to go through the pretence of collecting so-called evidence. Their indifference to truth lacked even its own callous inner logic.

He ate a scrappy breakfast. He was drinking his second cup of coffee when the doorbell rang.

He felt a violent revulsion in his stomach, then was angry with himself for being unprepared. If they had come, they had come. He went to the door.

It was the woman from the flat below. She looked at him half angrily, half fearfully. He wondered if she was going to complain about the noise he had made shifting furniture in the middle of the night. Then he remembered the hole, and the snapped wire, and he nearly grabbed her by the throat to shake the truth out of her.

She said: 'Ah, Professor Melisek.' She tried to peer past him. Of course she must know that Blanka had gone; perhaps had even watched her leave. 'I don't like to ask you, but . . . I wonder if . . . ' She was not a fluent liar. 'Are you going away?' she blurted out.

'Going away?'

She was more scared than he had been when he found the bug. She didn't know what had happened, but she was afraid she was going to be blamed for whatever had gone wrong.

'So many people are leaving,' she said. 'We . . . I wondered if you would be off to England.'

'Now?' He wasn't going to yield an inch.

'It's hard to know what to do. I thought . . . if you were going . . . you might take a letter for me.'

'A letter?'

'If you're going anywhere, or know some-one, or . . . Perhaps a letter you would carry. Nothing wrong, of course . . . '

'Of course not.'

She had a husband with all those contacts in the Foreign Office, and she wanted to know if he, Jan Melisek, might just happen to be going to England? A likely story. What were diplomatic bags for, anyway?

'I'm sorry,' he said. 'No.'

She wasn't sure whether he meant he wasn't going or that he would not take a letter.

She said: 'You're . . . not thinking of leaving?'

'Why should I? I've done no wrong.'

'Of course not. Goodness, no. I didn't mean — '

'I'm sorry.' He shut the door on her.

As he had said to her, he had done no

wrong. And as he had said to Blanka in Vienna, it had never really occurred to him that he might choose to stay permanently out of his own country. But at this moment he knew it was time to leave . . .

Gould said: 'And naturally you chose England, Professor.'

'Naturally. I have done a lot of work here. I feel at home here.'

'It is the place where you can be most useful,' said Gould bleakly.

There was a tap at the door. A uniformed man came in and put a sheet of paper and what looked like a fountain pen on the table. When he went out he closed the door with a resounding click. Jones drew the new items closer to his little hoard, but stabbed a thumb at the paper so that Gould would look at it.

Their heads bent over the sheet. Then Gould reached past it, selected a scrap of paper from the rest of the heap and waved it at Jan.

'Where did you get this?'

Jan leaned forward. Then he remembered. Nostalgia in a blur of mauve ink.

'That was when I was over last year, at a conference.'

'Where was the conference?'

'In Cambridge.'

'What were you doing on the Norwich branch line out of Ipswich, then? And which branch was it?'

'I . . . ' He thought of the job he had been ordered to do for Veselka. Oh no, he said silently: it was getting immeasurably worse. 'I had a day to spare. I went for a trip.'

There was another scrap of paper. Jones had been toying with it while Gould spoke. Now he said: 'These addresses in Orford — the addresses of friends?'

'No.'

'Then . . . ?'

'All right.' They were waiting for him to throw up his hands and confess all. But there was nothing to confess. 'They were given to me by the man I told you about — Veselka.'

'The one you said you refused to work for.'

'I did refuse. I didn't do what he wanted.'

'Which was what?'

'Oh, this bit of it was finding out details about those houses. Positions, price, owners and so on.'

'And so on. Including some views of the establishment on Orford Ness?'

'That didn't arise. And I didn't play, in any case.'

'You surely didn't go all that way and change your mind when you got there?'

'Oddly enough, it could look like that. But I didn't really mean to co-operate from the start.'

'A bit unsatisfactory all round, one would say?'

'Really, do I *look* like a spy?'

'Spies never look like spies,' said Gould. 'Our job would be so much easier if they did.'

Jones turned the larger sheet towards Jan. 'And this one?' he invited.

It was a typed list of names, with a few inked-in comments alongside some of them. Jan had never seen it before.

'I don't know,' he said.

Jones thrust it closer as though to force an admission from him. Jan glanced down the list. One name was that of a colleague in the Institute, another that of a volatile young researcher from the Institute of Agriculture whom he had met a couple of times.

'Does it mean anything now?'

'No.'

'Then what was it doing in your suitcase?'

Jan stared. 'In my suitcase?'

'The larger one. Slipped in behind the lining. But I'm sure you don't need telling that.'

'And this,' said Gould. They were feinting at him from both sides now, confident that one telling blow would land perfectly within a few seconds. Gould was prodding the pen towards him.

'That paper,' said Jan, 'whatever it is: it must have been planted. Or . . . ' But he had no alternative to offer.

'And this, too,' Gould persisted. 'This was planted?'

Jan picked up the pen. It meant nothing to him. They seemed to expect something of him, so automatically he unscrewed it in the middle, where one would fit a new cartridge or find the refill plunger.

A tiny, slim roll of film dropped into his palm.

'Neat,' said Jones. 'Very neat. Your boys are really brilliant when they get down to it.'

'You can't seriously imagine — '

'I'll tell you one thing, Professor,' said Gould with abrupt, breathtaking brutality. 'I think they made a bit of a cock-up when they picked you. I think you're just not up to the job.'

'A point I made to them at the time.' As Gould and Jones exchanged quizzical glances, Jan went over to the attack. 'What made you pick me out? It couldn't have been at random.'

'Professor, we are empowered to use our discretion in selecting immigrants for routine questioning.'

'Routine? It couldn't have been pure chance. You were tipped off I was coming. You were told what to look for. It's a trap: it has to be.'

Gould shrugged. Jones grinned complacently.

'Who?' Jan demanded. 'Who was it?'

An agent camouflaged as a refugee could easily have got here ahead of him and leaked the necessary accusations. The present crisis offered golden opportunities for infiltration.

He read the message in those disillusioned eyes. That was how they saw *him*: a potential mischief-maker.

He said: 'You can't seriously think — '

'Shall I tell you what we do think, Professor?'

'A Russian spy.' Jan laughed resignedly.

'Not at all. In your way you're a genuine refugee. But it's not the Russians you're running from, is it? It's your own people.'

'If you mean the S.T.B. — '

'We know all about the clique who tried to issue a semi-official invitation to the Russians. We know all about the telex messages that failed to get through, so that the invasion had to take place without even the concocted excuse. You were waiting for the pay-off . . . but it hasn't been what you expected, has it? Somebody rumbled you. It hasn't been

261

the walkover you expected. You had to clear out fast.'

'Insane,' whispered Jan.

'You want to sit tight over here and wait till your bosses have got things under control. And you've brought your list with you. Checking on those who may already have fled here. Waiting for them if they haven't shown up yet. Ready to report back when the day of reckoning comes.'

It was no good. No good arguing. No good even thinking.

It was the ultimate irony. Veselka had played the cruellest trick of all.

'Linz,' he said. 'That was it. That's what it was all about. Not taking something out of the car, but putting something *in*.'

A hasty, on-the-spot improvisation to make sure that his name was dirtied in England so that he would be sent back to Prague.

Surely there were other scapegoats, easier to round up when the time came? He was no special use and no special danger to Veselka . . . was he?

There was still that map. Handing it over to the girl had been an impetuous thing to do. But so many impetuous things must have been done during those muddled days. People hiding money, burying things, closing their front doors and setting off for distant countries; or tossing petrol bombs into tanks, scrawling slogans on walls.

Throwing pistols into dustbins, he thought wryly.

He had an excuse to see Maggie again, to reclaim his property. Remembering her crooked, discerning little smile, he wanted to provoke it again; but in fresh, gayer circumstances.

Western women are promiscuous by nature, I think?

The memory of Veselka's prurience couldn't contaminate this.

If ever he got past these two watch-dogs . . .

'We're glad to offer asylum to those escaping from the Russians,' said Gould; 'not to men working *for* them.'

10

Anthony Finch said: 'I really don't feel we ought to meddle. I mean, there's none of that bright lights and beating up sort of thing in this country. He'll get a fair hearing.'

Finch must have been to the barber that very morning. He gave off a faint aroma of coal tar shampoo, topped by some sweeter, more pungent lotion. His grey curls were glossy against the background of books with colourful spines. To his right, by the door, was a large chart pinned to a board. Twice while they had been talking there had been a tap at the door and a lean girl with glasses had come in and said, 'Sorry, sir,' and Finch had said, 'That's all right, Flora, go ahead,' and Flora had stuck a flag into the chart and gone out, and Finch had said, 'Marvellous girl, Flora — the place just wouldn't run without her.'

Just above Finch's blobby little right

ear, Maggie saw a book with Jan Melisek's name on it.

She said: 'They ought to have let him go by now.'

'Perhaps they have. We might get word at any time. I imagine he'll contact me first.'

'What about his cousin — he said something about having a cousin here.'

'Oh, I don't think he'd go there. Very tactless if he did. Wouldn't want to spoil the chap's chances.'

'Chances?'

'He's got to be very careful in that job of his. And he's in line for an M.B.E.'

'That's so important?' said Maggie.

'It's the most he can hope for,' said Finch, misunderstanding her, 'at his executive level.'

'But . . . '

There was a tap at the door. This time when Flora came in she was bearing a tray on which stood a large silver teapot, a teacup and saucer, and a monumental mug with an ornate design all round it.

'Thank you, Flora. Leave it on the corner of the desk. I'll be mother.'

Flora went out. Finch poured tea for Maggie, and then filled the mug. He turned it halfway round so that Maggie could admire it.

There was a garland of flowers painted all round the rim, and below that a number of sylvan scenes, accompanied by a black-lettered verse which was too curlicued for Maggie to read.

'It's appalling, isn't it?' said Finch proudly. 'It's *so* dreadful that one simply has to adore it.'

He buried his nose in the mug and drank.

Maggie said: 'You've known him a long time?'

'Melisek? Oh yes. Worked for five or six years with him, on two books. Never made much money out of them, but we're happy to publish him. Distinguished scholar — highest integrity.'

'Yes,' said Maggie firmly.

'I meant as a scholar. A bit earnest, you know — some of these specialists, these Central Europeans . . . ' She waited for him to say something about the wogs beginning at Calais. She bristled. He sensed it, and glanced at her in alarm over the rim of the mug. He gulped a scalding mouthful, and said hastily: 'A splendid chap. First-rate. It's just a matter of . . . um . . . sense of proportion.'

'If you're asked, you'll vouch for him?'

'If I were approached for, as it were, a reference, of course I'd say everything I know about him.'

'You don't sound too sure,' Maggie accused him.

'Well, one has to be scrupulously fair. A sense of proportion,' he repeated. It was evidently a reassuring incantation. 'What do we really know of what goes on over there? A chap can be a great conductor, or a geologist or a physicist, or whatever, and still play along — join the Party, that sort of thing — just to make things easier for himself. It's understandable. But we can't have that sort of thing encroaching on us, now can we?'

'You mean you think Jan — '

'My dear, I've known him a long time, as I've said. I like him. Like him enormously. But I can't honestly say that I know how he'd stand as a security risk.

The nicest of them probably have to do all manner of things they'd prefer not to. But' — he saw she was going to speak, and intercepted her — 'I'm sure it'll all be settled the right way. Those fellows know what they're doing, and if they decide — '

'So you're going to do nothing.'

Finch put his empty mug regretfully back on the tray. 'I could . . . um . . . make a few inquiries from a chap in my Club. But I shall have to tread gently. It wouldn't really be right for me to stir things up.'

Maggie put her cup also on the tray. She stood up. Finch pushed his leather-padded chair back and came round the desk to her.

'Don't be despondent,' he said, taking her hand and holding it with avuncular fervour. 'Can you leave me an address? The moment I have any news, I'll phone. And I'm sure . . . sure' — he squeezed her hand — 'that it'll be good news.'

She gave him the phone number of her flat and that of the Chinnery Group.

At the start she had meant to tell him about the map. Not to go into too much detail — just to say that she had something connected with Professor Melisek's work, and what ought she to do with it? In her own mind it had, really, been her excuse for going to see Finch. But it had somehow not cropped up when they began talking; and now she was obscurely glad. She would keep it until she could hand it over personally to Jan. Soon. It must be soon.

From the flat — three brightly aseptic rooms in Putney which not even her pictures, magazines, scatter cushions and scattered belongings could convert to homeliness — she telephoned her mother.

Mrs Armitage's lament came clear and lachrymose from the northern fringe of Essex. 'So you're back. Margaret, I've been so worried. Worried sick.'

'Well, it's all right now. Safely home.'

'I said all along you should never have gone.'

'Yes.' Margaret remembered only too well.

'I've been sitting by the phone waiting for some word. I was sure something awful had happened.'

'Mummy, I only got back last night.'

'Last night. And you didn't even think to ring and tell me you were all right?'

'I did think. I tried three times.'

'You didn't even give me a thought.'

'Three times,' said Maggie. 'There was no answer.'

'Nonsense.' Then Mrs Armitage said irritably: 'Oh, I was at Betty's playing bridge. I had to do *something* to keep my mind off things.'

'Playing at quarter past eleven?'

'We talked. I couldn't face coming home to another sleepless night.'

'Well, you can relax now,' said Maggie. 'I'm back.'

'I don't suppose I shall see you for ages.'

Maggie's heart sank. The house had meant so much to her when it was her grandmother's, but had never been the same since her mother took over. Patiently she said: 'I'll come down at the weekend.'

'Not before then?'

'I'll have to get things straightened out, and report to Mrs Chinnery.'

'Hmph,' said her mother. 'Yes, of course. Mrs Chinnery.'

'I do work for her, you know.'

'I never did like the idea.'

Maggie was glad when the conversation could decently be terminated. She collected a bundle of dirty clothes for the launderette, and then felt that she simply couldn't go out today. They would have to wait until tomorrow evening. Today she would wash her hair, watch television — whatever ghastly ravings might be on, she'd watch — and go to bed early.

At seven o'clock the doorbell chimed, just as she had fixed the last curler in position. Maggie cursed and debated whether to sit quite still and not make a sound. Then she thought it must be Jan — that somehow he had been in touch with Anthony Finch, had got her address and hurried round here — and she clawed a silk scarf over her head and went to the door.

Arnold said: 'You wriggled through their fiendish clutches! I must say, they went to a lot of trouble to net you — but you got away, hey?'

He was always shyly boisterous for his first few sentences, but then would calm down.

'Arnold,' she said. 'Come in.'

He kissed her, and aimlessly patted her behind.

'Knew you were back,' he said. 'Strolling along with my head in the air — makes a change, I was getting a crick in the neck from studying the pavement for fag-ends — and saw your colourful shape flitting across the bathroom window. So, old voyeur that I am, I thought I'd come for a closer look.'

He plonked himself down at one end of the couch. Always the same end. Even as he asked, 'Well, what was it like?' he was groping for the occasional table with its heavy glass ashtray, and tapping powder from his pipe before relighting it.

Maggie's everyday life was reasserting itself with a callous indifference to everything she had seen these last few days. There had been some panicky hours when London had seemed unreal and unattainable. Now Prague was a receding foreign trouble-spot where things happened to other people. Here she was in her familiar flat with her hair in curlers, Arnold was smoking his pipe and looking at her with fond, mild grey eyes; tomorrow she'd be back in the turmoil with which Mrs Chinnery loved to be surrounded, and at the weekend her mother would be waiting for her at Losspenny. It was the dependable routine through which she could move without needing to test every step. No alien perils at street corners, no signposts gone astray, no maps without meaning.

She told Arnold what it had been like, and found she was listening to her own story with mounting incredulity.

He nodded. 'Must have been bloody. Poor Mags.'

His head sank back against the cushion. He smiled with that grave attentiveness which could be so reassuring. He had thick, exuberant black eyebrows, but kept his hair puritanically short and neat. This evening he looked agreeably untidy and comfortable: he was wearing his oldest brown corduroys, rubbed thin at the knees where his landlady's cat liked to pummel him.

Maggie had met him four years ago while interviewing C.N.D. demonstrators for an American magazine survey. Even then he had seemed older and, attractively, more melancholy than most of his companions. His bony face, ascetic without being too cadaverous, seemed to have accumulated in its lines not merely several years more of life but a lot more disillusionment.

He was an architect in a hard-working partnership in Fulham. There had been talk of his setting up a provincial office somewhere in the North-West, but somehow it never materialised. With Arnold, Maggie was to discover, things had a habit of not quite coming to fruition; yet there was nothing feeble about him, and she could not have done without him just after her grandmother's death. There had been a time when she had thought he was going to take her to bed, and she had wanted to go. Then it hadn't happened, and somehow it was all right — she was still thankful to know that he was there. Once he had talked of buying a house, and gradually the implication had arisen that it would be shared with Maggie. They had gone so far as to look at some Chelsea houses, and one in Canonbury, and his professional enthusiasm created new possibilities in every house, every room. If Maggie had encouraged him, the project might well have gone ahead. She didn't know quite why she had let it slide.

Her mother liked him because he was polite, amusing, and invariably asked after her health, making her feel that two or three of her ailments were rather unusual and of some scientific interest. From time to time she asked Maggie when she was going to marry Arnold. 'It hasn't actually cropped up,' Maggie would say. Each time the question was asked she felt mildly surprised — and yet that somehow they might very well, one day, marry. Put like that it sounded tame; yet she was very fond of Arnold, and there had never been anyone else of any great consequence.

'And you?' she asked when she had finished her account. 'What have you been up to while I've been away?'

'I dropped in at a summer school last week. Some bright young students there. A splendid crowd, some of them, you know — a lot more imaginative in their thinking than I was at their age. I think there's going to be a big shake-up in some of the universities this next year or so. There's a new social conscience. I promised I'd help with a demonstration next term.'

'And Czechoslovak demonstrations?' Maggie asked. 'I hope you're keeping them up?'

'Keeping them up?'

'I haven't had a chance to see the papers — I'm a bit behindhand with the news. I've been too busy,' she observed, 'getting myself out of the news where it's really happening. But I suppose you had some kind of march on Sunday?'

Arnold frowned slightly. She thought perhaps he was criticising her choice of words: he had been a marcher in the Aldermaston days, but nowadays tended more to sit down wherever there was a bit of pavement free.

'Well,' he said, 'a few of the boys did go along to Kensington Palace Gardens. But we've been rather busy with a Vietnam demo.'

'Another one?'

'Do you realise' — he pushed himself upright — 'the Americans don't *want* to make progress at the Paris talks. It's all been a sham. They make a pretence of showing willing, and continue to escalate the attack. Their conceit won't let them give in. They're hurt, so they want to hurt back — a million times over. Have you seen their own predictions?'

'I — '

'No, of course, you haven't seen the papers for ages. Their *own* predictions — another hundred thousand dead over the next two years. Their own dead, mind you. Just figures on a balance sheet. Anything rather than let the Vietnamese rule their own country.'

'Yes,' said Maggie. 'Just what the Czechs are facing at the moment.'

'I don't know that I'd go that far.'

'You wouldn't?'

'You've got to be objective about this,

love. Got to see it — '

'I've seen it. I'm just back from seeing it.'

'Yes, yes. I know how it is.' Arnold's fervour abated slightly. He sucked his pipe and narrowed his eyes judicially through a blue drift of smoke. 'The immediate impact of an experience like that must make it temporarily impossible to stand back and take in the broader picture.'

'You think so?'

'One does have to respect the Russian viewpoint. Of course the invasion was a mistake. Clumsy and ill-conceived.'

Maggie was aghast. 'That's all you can find to say about it?'

'Do try to take all the factors into consideration,' said Arnold seriously. 'The Russians lost millions of dead when the Germans overran their country. They may be a bit overwrought about Western Germany today, but you can hardly blame them for not wanting a disaffected, disruptive Westernised state on their doorstep. And really, was this wonderful Czech renaissance so very wonderful, when you get down to it? They didn't seem to have any clear long-term policy. They'd just been listening too gullibly to American and German propaganda. I'm not trying to justify the Russians, but — '

'It sounds awfully like it,' said Maggie.

'I'm sorry you can't assess it without prejudice.'

He sounded so gentle and tolerant. She had known him to be scrupulously fair like this before, jumping on an extreme end of a moral seesaw to readjust the balance and succeeding in bringing it down with a bang.

For once she could not endure another word. 'My hair,' she said. 'Arnold, I really must settle down under the dryer.'

He tapped his pipe in the ashtray. 'Of course, you must have a lot to do. Sorry I barged in.' When she saw him to the door, he said: 'I'll let you know the general set-up of the Vietnam protest.'

'Do that.'

'Any chance of you coming along on Sunday?'

'I'll be out in the sticks on Sunday, seeing Mummy.'

'Give her my love.'

After he had gone, while she leaned at an awkward angle under her wobbly table hair-dryer, she tried to follow his advice and be objective. Most of the time she found she was thinking of Jan and wondering where he was and how they could get in touch again.

'Holidays in Britain,' intoned Mrs Chinnery in her best prophetess manner. 'That's something we can concentrate on.'

Maggie felt herself being drawn a few degrees further into the old familiar ambience. Mrs Chinnery was wearing a flamboyant new dress in the best psychedelic style, all whorls of mauve, angelica, shocking pink and off-orange; but her complexion, though matching one fashionable new shade, was the same, and her voice was the same, and the wide teak desk and the blown-up cartoon frame on the wall and the arc of dutiful listeners were all the same.

'Never believe it. You won't. But there he was — out of the top kennel in the British Travel and Holidays lot — and what do you think he said? I was telling him what Piet said. Remember Piet, Robin?'

'Piet was Charlie's customer, not mine.'

'Yes. I told this oaf. Told him what our charming little Dutchman had said. Useful advice, I'd have thought. Why is it that there's nowhere in England where holidaymakers can go, the way they do on the Continent, and the man has a beer — wife has cup of coffee — daughter has Coke and a cream cake, or something. Why? Nothing like a French or Austrian café. Absolutely nothing. Where *can* visitors go? You know what this man said? You know?'

They waited respectfully during her protracted dramatic pause.

'He said to me,' Mrs Chinnery declared with solemn relish, 'he said, 'There's always the Dorchester.' And he meant it. He really couldn't *see!*'

She spoke in a clipped voice, sometimes discarding syllables and sometimes whole words as though she were a tweedy wife from the hunting counties or a retired W.R.A.C. officer. In fact she was known to be the illegitimate daughter of a Fleet Street tycoon who had bought her quietly into a small advertising agency in the hope that it would keep her quiet, and was now alarmed by her progress and what he heard of her methods.

'If we want the Germans and the French and the Scandinavians to spend their money here,' she said, 'we've got to offer them what they want. The Spaniards cater for the English taste — they're not too proud to build fish and chip shops all down their coastline. We've got to do the same. Not enough research has been done. And that' — she sat back and smiled the hard-edged pillar-box smile they recognised as the announcement of a new campaign — 'is our next task. Survey of coastal resorts. Cafés, restaurants, boarding-houses. Structured interviews first, then some snooping. And Maggie, I think you'll be the one to go round all the national travel agencies. Sound 'em out. Get 'em to joke about it — and then take it seriously. And when we're stoked up . . .'

One of her three telephones rang. Mrs Chinnery looked at it as she might have looked at a pet parrot which had dared to think up a new phrase for itself.

Robin, who was sitting nearest, reached for the receiver, but she snatched it up herself.

'I gave strict instructions . . . '

She listened. Then glared at Maggie. Then said: 'Oh. Just a minute.'

The others carefully did not look at Maggie.

Mrs Chinnery said: 'It's a Mr Finch. Some publisher or something. Says it's urgent. If you'd like to take it out in the — '

But Maggie's knees were already wedged against the desk. She took the phone from Mrs Chinnery's large pink hand and said: 'Yes. Maggie Armitage.'

Anthony Finch's voice said: 'That matter of that friend of ours.'

'Yes. You've heard from him?'

'He . . . um . . . can you possibly come round here at once?'

'Well . . . ' Maggie glanced at Mrs Chinnery, who was studiously not listening. 'Perhaps later — '

'Couldn't you possibly come now?' He was whispering, as though international secrets were at stake. 'I . . . um . . . it would be such a help.'

Mrs Chinnery said abruptly: 'If it's something urgent, Maggie, do buzz off.'

'May I?'

'What am I?' demanded Mrs Chinnery. 'A dragon?'

'I'll be right round,' said Maggie, and put the phone down. She tried hurriedly to explain. 'It's rather weird — something about something I brought home from Prague — '

'Spare us the details,' said Mrs Chinnery. 'I might feel obliged to notify the Customs bods. Now get cracking.' But as Maggie reached the door, she said: 'Finch. Not Farrell and Finch?'

'Finch and Farrell.'

'Exactly. Publishers. Glad you're establishing contacts of that kind, Maggie. Might mention a little idea of mine. Study of research techniques for top management. Comprehensive. Crying need for it.'

'I'll try to — '

'Relate it to our other activities. Perhaps issue it as part of the package we offer to clients. Well, drop the notion in the feller's In-tray. And now,' said Mrs Chinnery benevolently, 'do hurry along.'

Maggie hurried. She found a taxi, and fumed in it for twenty minutes through traffic jams.

She was shown into Anthony Finch's office by Flora, who closed the door behind her.

Jan was getting to his feet as she came in. He put out both hands, and she held them and they both laughed for some reason, and then he kissed her.

Anthony Finch coughed and said: 'I want to make it quite plain that I can't allow myself to be mixed up in this. It would be wrong. Quite wrong.'

11

They were together in the Renault again. The roads here were not as pitted and uneven as those of Bohemia. Signposts were decorously in place, though Maggie had no need of them. She hummed to herself as she drove out towards Eastern Avenue and the A12.

Jan sat quiet until they were clear of the worst of the traffic. Then he said: 'You will be sorry you ever met me.'

'Funny,' said Maggie, 'I was thinking how nice it was to have you there again. Brightens up the whole day.'

'It was Finch I went to for help. It was Finch I thought would do something.'

'And now you know,' said Maggie cheerfully.

'If I'd thought of the trouble I would cause, perhaps I would not have jumped off that train.'

'He who hesitates, and all that.'

The hell with them, Maggie was

thinking with childish exhilaration. The hell with all of them: the squares, the creeps, the dead-from-the-neck-upwards lot. Like Jan, she hadn't thought it out in detail. It had simply been a matter of 'Right, let's go.' Jump! Even the thought of her mother's inevitable reproaches didn't deter her.

'It was mad,' he said, 'but I couldn't bear the feeling of them closing in on me. Here they are polite to the accused, and still it is terrifying . . . the hand tightening, choking the breath out of you . . . '

They had said there must be further questions. A colleague in London would like to interview this Professor Melisek. Jan got the impression that, in spite of their confident condemnation, they were worried by the flatfootedness of the Orford episode. Somewhere there must be a complicated double bluff. 'Nothing can ever be what it seems,' he observed to Maggie. 'For them there must always be half-truths and deceptions, turns and twists. Nothing simple.' So he was asked if he would mind going to London; as though he had any choice.

He would be well looked after, he was assured. If it was finally decided that he could not be allowed to stay in England, he would be put back on a plane as soon as normal civil flights to Prague were resumed. They intimated that there was no likelihood of their putting him back on the boat and returning him to Calais: he could make quite a nuisance of himself, making sorties from French or Belgian ports. A plane direct to Prague was the answer.

'But they're bound to find out at the other end,' Jan protested. 'There'll be someone waiting for me.'

They seemed to have anticipated this, and it gave them a certain pleasure. 'That's your lookout, isn't it? Not ours.'

He travelled on the London train with two plain-clothes men in a special compartment. Did they have a permanent reservation, always ready for suspected immigrants?

It was not how he had planned to arrive in England. Not how he had planned to go to London.

Perhaps the inquisitor in London would see sense. Once his story had been analysed, they must see that it was true.

They couldn't send him back. Couldn't soullessly deliver him back to the waiting Veselka.

Yet if Veselka was really waiting, had really implicated him in this grisly charade, why hadn't he pounced earlier? There had been several days in Prague when Jan could have been snared, if Veselka had wanted him. If. And if not, if Blanka . . .

The same old questions, still going round and round in his head and making no rhyme or reason.

The two men in the compartment with him were neither chatty nor hostile. They seemed content to be where they were, occasionally looking out of the window, offering him a cigarette every now and then.

Jan got up to go to the lavatory. At once the heavier of the two was at the door, blocking the corridor one way. He walked along with Jan, and was waiting outside when Jan came out.

The train was slowing. It was an express to London, but as it emerged from a tunnel it slackened speed over points, and coasted in gently beside a station platform. Then there was a jolt like a sudden hiccup, and it began to gather speed again.

Jan was facing a door. The platform slid past invitingly.

He didn't think. He opened the door, and jumped.

There was a yell behind him, snatched away under the stone arch of a road bridge. Jan hurried along the platform. There was another shout as a porter appeared and bustled towards him.

If he had stopped to doubt, or to choose a way out of this utterly strange place, he might have been caught. He was tired of running away — and yet he was driven on. An inspector said, 'Now just a minute,' and was shouldered aside. Somebody tried to swing a door shut in his face. He charged at it, was through, and then found himself running up a slope. The shouts from behind were drowned by a whistle as a train approached from the other direction, and there was a resonant howl and clatter of a diesel under the bridge. He had the presence of mind to slow his pace as he reached the top of the station approach, and to walk idly past a group of youngsters on the corner. He made himself keep up this steady pace until he was sure, in a side street, that there was no pursuit.

He was in a town called Sevenoaks. He bought a cheap suitcase, a razor and a shaving-brush — 'Again!' he said to Maggie as he told the story — and that night found a hotel on a country road just outside the town. In the morning he discovered that there was a long-distance coach service running through Sevenoaks from the coast to London. He booked a seat.

'And here I am.'

'Yes,' said Maggie, 'here you are.'

Beyond Chelmsford she swung off due north, and after twenty minutes approached the familiar turning for Losspenny.

'Your family home, this?' Jan ventured.

'Not one of the stately homes, if that's what you're hoping for. Wait till you see it.'

They passed the sagging iron gates of the old manor. One gatepost was cracking diagonally, and moss had turned the lower sections of the ironwork green. The manor was a grey hulk between the trees.

The road skirted a pond, as green as the mossy gates. On its far side a tree trunk was warped into the shape of a crouching, petrified giant with three arms.

Maggie slowed for the abrupt turn-off on to the lane, over the ruts and up to the house.

It was an old farmhouse to which a square brick frontage had been added in Victorian times, together with a large conservatory at the southern end. Even from a distance, seen through the hedge and the trees, it could not claim to be picturesque. It was large and inconvenient. Along the north side was a passage no more than a yard wide, flanked by a high brick wall which cut out light from the downstairs windows. It was clogged with wet leaves. Maggie had loved the dank smell along there, and had found a mysterious tranquillity in the sombre rooms on that side of the house. Once upon a time — before her grandmother died.

Now there was her mother, grumbling round the place, resenting everything that life had done to her.

Mrs Armitage had been widowed when Maggie was only five. They lived in Peterborough and came to Losspenny for holidays — 'Because we can't afford to go anywhere else,' Maggie's mother had told her friends, and Maggie, and any of Maggie's friends who so much as mentioned going to Yarmouth or Scarborough or — unforgivably — Spain, Greece or anywhere over the water.

Maggie wasn't sorry they couldn't afford anywhere else. She liked the decrepit house with its light and shade, its innumerable smells, its abandoned rooms with peeling rosebud wallpaper, and its creaks and squeaks and mutterings.

'It's hateful,' said her mother. 'Detestable.'

When she was eight, Maggie asked if she could live for ever in Losspenny with her grandmother. Her mother took this as a personal slight. 'Just because she spoils you outrageously . . . what an unnatural thing to think of . . . '

But Mrs Armitage the elder did not, in fact, spoil Maggie. She was a sharp-tongued, severe, rigidly upright old woman with bright blue eyes and a tiny mouth which could have been mean but wasn't. Her clothes swished and rustled in a way which was to echo in Maggie's mind for years. What Maggie most cherished was being treated as an adult. There had never been a time when her grandmother condescended or talked down to her. They argued by the hour. 'Giving the child ideas,' snorted her mother. This, possibly, was what rankled most: the old lady treated her own daughter as a fractious child, but spoke to her grand-daughter as to an equal.

When she was at L.S.E., Maggie had brought a rather important boy-friend to Losspenny for a weekend. It would not have occurred to her to offer him to her mother for inspection at this stage. A few months later — even a few weeks later — she had difficulty in recalling why he had ever seemed important; but at the time she had wanted to get some glimmering of her grandmother's reaction.

She was shocked to find her in crippling pain. The shrewd brown, puckered face had gone grey save for the lips, which were frighteningly purple. They talked, but for once the old lady was not concentrating. She held on to herself with a harrowing effort.

Maggie took her guest to the local pub, phoned her mother, and insisted that somebody ought to be here, in the house. Her mother made a fuss, but agreed to come the day after Maggie and the young man had gone back to London.

Ten days later the old lady died. Maggie was not notified of the funeral until it was over.

'I didn't want you to have to go through all that rigmarole,' her mother said in bleak self-righteousness. 'Didn't want to interrupt your studies — not after what they're costing.'

Maggie was desolated. It was unthinkable that her grandmother should have gone off without a word, with no bridge between that last meeting and this nothingness.

Her grandmother had been a severe Christian, steadily believing, but willing to argue with Maggie. Maggie had been by turns Church of England, a dabbler in Christian Science, spiritualism and Buddhism, and ultimately an agnostic. It was not until her grandmother's death that she realised how, deep down, she had somehow trusted fate to play fair: whatever her own beliefs or disbeliefs, her grandmother had relied on God and should therefore have been carried gently over into death. Instead, she had been racked and broken. The devouring cancer had gnawed out from within, literally destroying her backbone.

'It was dreadful, right at the end,' said Maggie's mother. 'I'm glad you weren't there.' And later she had repeated it, with embellishments: 'She didn't know what to do with herself. It's a blessing you weren't there. You'd thank me, if you knew. You wouldn't have been able to stand it.'

Maggie hadn't understood how her mother could move so promptly into the house, after all she had said against it. But, 'It's been left to me, and heaven knows we need to *save*,' said Mrs Armitage; and, 'I thought you adored the place — you were always going on about living here for ever.'

Now Maggie hated to come here. Yet here she was again, bringing someone else. Not so young this time. And there was no grandmother to pout dry lips and grimace apparent disapproval. When her mother's lips tightened it was in unadulterated peevishness, not because of an inner torment too great to be borne.

★   ★   ★

Maggie said: 'Mummy, this is Professor Melisek. Jan Melisek.'

'Oh.' Mrs Armitage extended a reluctant hand. 'I didn't know you'd be bringing somebody with you. If you'd told me, I could have aired — '

'It's been a dreadful scurry,' said Maggie. 'Jan is from Czechoslovakia. A Czech refugee.'

'Oh, yes. I've been hearing about them.'

Maggie led Jan into what her grandmother had always called the parlour and which would always be called the parlour. There was a rocking chair near the window, and a musty, faded armchair by the fireplace, commanding a view down the overgrown lawn. She made Jan sit down, and closed the door as she went out.

'Mummy, I want Professor Melisek to stay here for a week or two, until we sort one or two things out.'

'Sort things out? Margaret, there's nothing wrong, is there?'

'He's a refugee.' Maggie tried to give the word a mystical ring, to block any impious questions. 'He's a distinguished scholar, he's had to leave his own country fast, and he'll need a permit to stay here. I'm going to fix things for him. But you're not to say a word to anyone, Mummy. All right?'

'Margaret, there isn't going to be any trouble? I couldn't bear any . . . unpleasantness. It's most thoughtless of you, really it is. We're not going to have any — '

'We're not going to have any anything,' said Maggie. 'Just keep quiet, that's all. And leave it to me.'

Her mother looked sullen, but made a pot of tea and produced some home-made scones.

Maggie showed Jan round the house. It was the first time since that catalytic death that the place had come to life again for her. Trying to make him see it through her eyes, she herself saw it again, as it had once been.

'Who says so?' The echo of her own younger, demanding voice echoed down the corridors. Her grandmother would sit in the rocker or in the ladder-backed chair by the entrance to the conservatory, and they would talk. And later, when there was no more talk, there would be Maggie's own solitary voice: 'I'll show them. *I'll* show them.'

She found that she was gripping Jan's

arm as she led him out of one room and into another. When they had reached the end of the tour, he said softly:

'We have little of this left in my country. Few homes with family memories. I think there was an unwritten decree, at some stage, that echoes should be liquidated.'

Mrs Armitage had appeared twice while they were making the rounds: once with a pillow and sheets in her arms, the second time carrying a bedside lamp with the flex and plug trailing behind.

She had put Jan in a room on the extreme eastern corner of the house, far away from Maggie's bedroom. It was as bad as the hotel in Linz, but here there wasn't even an apology.

When they were washing up after eating the crepinettes which Maggie had brought from Old Compton Street, Mrs Armitage raised another protest.

'If anybody comes asking about this Professor — '

'No one will come. Nobody knows he's here.'

'But if they find out?'

'I'm not going to tell anyone. Are *you*?'

'It's not right. You've no right to do this to me, Margaret.'

Rinsing a plate, Maggie thought about this. The impetus that had started her in this direction was gone. As Arnold might have recommended, she was beginning to see things objectively.

She said: 'No. I suppose I haven't. I'm sorry.'

Mrs Armitage was taken aback. 'Not that I'm saying your friend's not welcome, or anything.'

'No. I know you're not, Mummy. But there really isn't any reason why you should be mixed up in this. If you want us to make other arrangements, I don't blame you.'

'Where would you go?'

'Oh, we could find somewhere. I can ring a few friends. Someone'll rally round.'

'I wouldn't think of it,' said Mrs Armitage. 'He stays here.'

'Mummy, if anything *did* go wrong — '

'You said there wouldn't be any trouble.'

'There oughtn't to be. But just in case, I wouldn't want you to be involved.'

'Hmph,' said her mother.

It was as close as they would ever get, now, to any demonstration of affection or, as the only possible substitute, family solidarity.

That night Maggie lay awake and listened to the unsleeping rustle of the leaves outside her window. She knew every cadence, every sound in and around this house.

Jan didn't. Jan wouldn't dare to leave his room and come in search of her. Even if her mother was not actually lying there, alert, on horizontal sentry duty, the creak and scrape of boards would set off an alarm.

Maggie knew which boards creaked, where there was one step up, and where not to lean on the wall.

She got out of bed and stood by the window. There was no moon, but the pale night sky seemed to draw up a tremulous brightness from the earth. She could make out the silhouette of the church tower, and the copse at the end of the line. The tree by her window went on whispering provocatively at her.

Give it time, she told herself. Wait. All in good time.

But tomorrow they might be surrounded. By what? Policemen, Russians, traitorous Czechs dropped by parachute or smuggled across the Essex marshes . . .

She opened and closed her door silently, and went along the landing. Six inches that way there was a loose board. Four or five feet further on, you had to take a long stride, otherwise an unevenness in the flooring made one of the bedroom doors grate slightly against its jamb.

Here the step. Up and along, and then a slight squeak of her bare feet on the uncarpeted corner.

She stopped outside Jan's door. Ridiculous to tap and wait for him to ask her in. He might be asleep by now, anyway. She half turned, contemplating the return journey, with her warm bed at the end of it. Warm but getting colder, the longer she delayed.

She opened Jan's door and went in.

At least one of the doors in the house fitted better than she would have imagined. There had been no rim of light round this one, but when she went into the bedroom she found that Jan's bedside light was on and he was propped up in bed with bolster and pillow wedged behind him.

'Hello,' he said quietly. 'I thought I heard you coming.'

She looked at the old-gold lampshade, which didn't go with the faded room.

'Reading?' she said.

He held out his empty hands. 'I brought no books with me.'

When she reached the bed he leaned forward so that his hands were on her waist. He flinched as though he had been given a brief electric shock. Then he laughed, and Maggie laughed with him. She let herself fall farther towards him, and his hands slid up under her pyjama jacket until they took the weight of her breasts.

Their mouths met. His hands became urgent with a loving cruelty.

As he came into her, she reached for

the light switch. He laughed again, and knocked her hand aside. She was driven down into the bed. His shoulders were so broad that they blocked out the ceiling ... the whole world. But he pulled his head back and his eyes looked into hers, and he was no pedantic Professor Melisek, no student of skeletons but a lover of living flesh, looking deep into her and moving deeper into her. She wanted to say something now, right now, something true and funny. Dear Professor, your first demonstration of your thesis ...

Then she gasped and there were no words. She clung to him, silently begging that the pounding should stop, yet craving for it to go on. She pulled him down closer and closer, until her teeth were against his shoulder. Then in the last timeless moment he reared up again, and his eyes seemed to beat with the same pulse that throbbed inside her.

In the dawn, after they had slept and made love again and slept again, Jan said: 'And you are going to keep me incarcerated here, just for your personal use?'

'Not a bad idea,' said Maggie. 'In fact, it's a wonderful idea.'

'Yes. A better prison than I dared to expect.'

But as the morning light grew stronger on his face, she saw that he was staring remotely at the ceiling, with those eyes that had stared so intensely into hers. His hand, that had been lying on her thigh, slid away on to the bed.

'Don't go away!' She propped herself up on her elbow and looked down at him. 'Don't run away from *me*.'

12

Conditions for working on that great, definitive book of his — 'the big one,' as Anthony Finch referred to it — were surely favourable. He could shut himself away all day long, every day, and not be disturbed. There was no Institute to go to. The view from his window was of flat, undistracting countryside. When his plea for asylum was eventually accepted, there would be a lot of work to do and he might have to put the book aside. Right now he ought to work on a first draft, and deal with the various sections in more painstaking detail when he had proper reference facilities.

'If you want me to bring you any books from London,' said Maggie, 'just shout. And I've got four library tickets.'

It was not until he came to scribble a basic list of titles he needed that he realised how many of them would be unobtainable in this country, and just how irreplaceable his collection in Prague was. When he could move freely, he would have to find ways of stocking up again. There might even be a way, when things had calmed down, of having the more important part of his library sent over here.

For the time being he was helpless. He waited for Maggie: waited for her to make inquiries, make contacts, 'stir it up', as she put it. But not stirring too vigorously. It was difficult to decide who to approach and how to get the problem taken seriously without leading the authorities straight to him. He could contribute nothing. He had to wait for her to find the right lead. He had to rely on her to bring books for him. And each day he waited for Maggie herself.

'She always used to stay in that flat of hers for weeks on end,' said Mrs Armitage accusingly. 'Didn't used to see her from one month to the next. Now I don't know whether she's coming or going.'

Some nights she stayed, as usual, in town. But at the end of most working days she drove out to Losspenny with news or no news. He could hear the car as it turned down the lane, and was at the door waiting to meet her. It was topsy-turvy, really, the man waiting in the house for the woman to come home, like a sick husband with a working wife; or, he thought, like a prisoner waiting for the reprieve to be brought.

Masterpieces had been written in prison. Few gaols had working conditions as comfortable as these.

Gaol. He tried to make a joke of it to himself.

Sometimes Maggie's eyes were tired, and then their flickering greenness darkened, and the shadows below them were like a sprinkling of dust. In sunlight her hair was russet. On a cloudy day, or late in the evening, it deepened to a matt brown — 'Like cheap brown paper,' she commented one night as he stroked it and turned her head gently towards the bedside light.

When they were together, in the light or the darkness, she shed her tiredness. Each time she brought no news from the outside world, he felt a sag of disappointment. Another day on his sentence. But then at night there were no barriers, and there was no time and no world outside her body.

Afterwards, when they talked, it was usually about her childhood, and then about his. Then, inexorably, they came up to date. She said she had been pestering Finch, and Jan said: 'You ought not to have to do that.' Finch had her London address, but she was not giving him the Essex one. 'Then there's your cousin,' she said one night. But Jan said, 'No, no, he is not the type. I think it would not be fair to upset the poor man.' She declared that she would upset the whole country, the whole smug lot of them, before she was finished. And then, half drowsy but ready to be reawakened, their voices would slur, and he would find he wanted to touch her again, and his fingers would begin their exploration all over again, and each time it was utterly new. He recited a litany of Maggie's beauty in Czech as he touched and kissed, and she laughed a protest — 'It's not fair, not fair, what are you *saying?'* — but her own hands and the rhythmic response of her body told him that she knew what he was saying.

Then in the morning she would be gone. 'Get some work done, and leave the rest to me.' But he got no work done. He read the newspapers and would have watched television news at every possible time but for Mrs Armitage's fidgeting, unhappy presence in the same room.

The papers were little consolation. There was a report that the best brains in the country had been advised to flee. He was lucky that he had chosen this course of action early on. But then there was a denial, and the assurance that things were not so bad after all.

The Russians were withdrawing in great numbers.

The Russians threatened to annihilate the country if they didn't get every one of their demands.

There was to be a Government reshuffle, introducing more, rather than less, liberal elements.

No. The old hard-liners were being reinstated due to Russian pressure.

Mrs Armitage accepted that Jan was to be permanently installed in the parlour. She brought his meals to him there, and when he suggested it would be much easier for her if he came out to the stone-flagged kitchen to eat, she backed away and did not so much protest as let the subject die into a resentful mumbling.

Once, abruptly, she said to him: 'Do you think my daughter knows what she's doing, Professor?'

It was a veiled accusation, like so many of her remarks. She wanted a confession from him. It was hard to blame her. Here, shut up with her under her own roof, was this foreigner, so much older than her daughter . . .

'Do any of us really know?' he hedged.

She said, 'Hmph,' and went off to a cupboard under the stairs. She hauled out a vacuum cleaner and trailed yards of serpentine hose behind her. Although he spoke English so fluently, she didn't really believe that it meant the same to him as it did to the true English: he couldn't be expected to grasp any subtlety she tried to convey.

One afternoon he crossed the cobbled yard that must once have been the farm-yard, and opened the gate on to the meadow. Mrs Armitage came scurrying after.

'You're not going out?'

'I need a breath of air.'

'But Maggie said you had to stay in. I'm sure you ought not to be wandering about.'

'I've got to walk,' he said, 'and think. I can't be cooped up all day. I need to walk: I've always done a lot of walking.'

He strode off towards a distant village, but did not actually go into it. He found some rutted lanes and made a long detour. Two cars, a lumbering cart and a tractor passed him. The tractor driver waved. A little girl skipped out through a farm gate and said, 'Hello,' and an elderly man plodding along the grass verge said, 'Art'noon.' He got back to Losspenny half an hour before Maggie drove under the old stable roof.

Mrs Armitage reported that he had been out.

'My dear' — Maggie leaned on his shoulder, her cheek cold against his

— 'did you *have* to?'

'Yes,' he said.

'It must be deadly, shut up all day. But hold tight. Don't panic. I think I've got Finch worried. Hopping a bit. He thinks he may be able to help.'

'I would like to think I can trust him.'

That night, with his arms round her, he said: 'I mustn't stay here much longer.'

'Here?' She drew him invitingly closer.

'In this house,' he said. 'It is wrong. For your mother, for you — wrong, all of it.'

'My darling, please be patient. Please.'

'They will find me sooner or later. I'm surprised they haven't already tried. They must have a record of your car, they'll know we were together, they will come to your flat in London and then they'll be down here — and there will be trouble for you.'

'Patience,' said Maggie. Then she said: 'But right now, perhaps I wouldn't say no to a little impatience in one direction.'

The next day he stayed indoors and jotted down a few notes. They didn't amount to much. He was cut off. Nothing was of any significance save Maggie. A romantic situation. An idyll. But he was not made to be merely a tame lover.

He wondered whether it would be best simply to walk away while she was in London. He could find the nearest station and disappear.

Running again? He would wait until Maggie came down, this evening or tomorrow, and tell her; and refuse to be argued out of it.

When the car arrived, it came up the lane with a wilder snarl than usual. It racketed across the yard and into the stable, and stopped with a screech of brakes.

Maggie got out and hurried him indoors. 'I'm sure I was followed. There was someone on my tail most of the way.'

'Let me leave now,' he said, 'before — '

'You'll stay here.'

A large black Wolseley turned into the lane. They watched it from the window. Mrs Armitage stood well back in the room. 'I knew all along,' she said. 'I knew it. I said all along.'

The fields beyond stretched to the flat horizon. Run, thought Jan wearily. Run and keep running till you came to the edge and could throw yourself over.

The car stopped, and a man got out. It was the one called Gould.

He studied the house and came up to the front door. There was the jangle of the bell wire in its rusty channel, and the rattle of the bell. Mrs Armitage stayed where she was, frozen.

Maggie said: 'Jan, go upstairs and stay there until — '

'No. I will open the door. I am the one he wants.'

Before she could protest he went to the door. Maggie hurried behind him.

Gould said: 'Miss Armitage. Professor. May I come in?'

Jan stood back. Gould walked past him without a tremor, ruling out any possibility of being struck over the head from behind.

'You needn't have driven quite so fiercely, Miss Armitage,' he said. 'We had a pretty good idea of the locality anyway. We'd have got here eventually.'

'The planes are flying again?' said Jan. 'You're ready to toss me back in?'

'That's not the idea at all. You really ought not to have bolted like that, Professor. If only you'd given us time, you'd have found us very reasonable people. Very reasonable. I've come here to tell you' — it came out with amiable disapproval, as though Gould would have preferred to deliver a quite different verdict — 'that we accept your story.'

Maggie sat down abruptly. Jan leaned against the back of her chair.

'Of course,' Gould went on, making the most of it, 'we *could* encourage the police to prefer charges against you — resisting arrest, escaping from custody — '

'Was there ever a formal charge against Professor Melisek?' asked Maggie.

Gould looked at her.

Mrs Armitage said: 'Margaret, I do wish you wouldn't show off. I'm sure this gentleman — '

'Let's not split hairs, Miss Armitage. I take your point, but I assure you there are several quite legitimate charges we could arrange to have made, particularly in view of the Professor's alien nationality. But we don't intend to do so.'

Jan took a deep breath and said: 'So I may stay?'

'You may stay, Professor. You will of course have to ask for regular extensions of your permit in the usual way. But I think there are unlikely to be any objections.'

'What made you decide I was . . . admissible?'

'Your story made more sense if it was true than if it was a fabrication,' said Gould. 'But more than that, we have had some flattering testimonials on your behalf. Other refugees have arrived. They speak highly of you. To be quite frank, they have such a high opinion of your integrity that we even began to wonder if you were not the most skilful espionage and counter-espionage practitioner in the business.' He allowed himself a wintry smile. 'But that didn't fit with our assessment of you. And then, one final bit of evidence which interested us. One of our opposite numbers in West Germany passed on some information. They picked up someone just like you — or, rather, someone who was just what he originally thought of *you*. A real sharp operator, this one. And he had a list of names, just like the one you were carrying. Only yours was incomplete. This character had the full one. And your own name was on it, Professor.'

'I was on their black list. Yes. I've known that all along.'

Gould said: 'What we'd still like to know is why they went to such trouble to incriminate you. None of the other refugees we've dealt with has been loaded with such stuff.'

Jan hesitated, then leaned over the chair close to Maggie's left ear, close to the warmth and scent of her neck and throat and her hair. 'I think he'd better see that map,' he said.

'Jan — '

'Yes. I think it would be best. You still have it?'

She got up. 'You're sure?' When he nodded, she went out of the room.

Gould said: 'Have you been withholding something from us, Professor?'

'Nothing that I felt legally or morally obliged to show you. But now that I'm here . . . now it's going to be permanent . . . I shall never know what it was all about unless you, or someone, can explain it.'

He summarised the story of the map. Still he held something back: he kept Blanka out of it, and would not have cared to justify his motives for this: a memory of humiliation, unwillingness to let Mrs Armitage know about Blanka, an attempt to strip the whole subject of misleading personal emotion?

Gould listened impassively. Mrs Armitage let out an occasional little gasp.

Maggie came back into the room and waited for Jan to finish. Then she handed the map to Gould.

'We'll have a look. I'll be in touch.'

As Gould turned away and left, Jan felt that another thread joining him to his country had snapped; that another part of his own self had been shredded away.

'So it's all right,' said Maggie. 'It's all right.'

★ ★ ★

It was all right.

He was free to move. Free to go to London, to re-establish his contacts with the School of Slavonic and East European Studies, to accept an advance from Finch and Farrell for the book — 'the big one' — now definitely commissioned, and to make it known that he was available for lectures.

He was invited to appear on a monthly television programme called *Facts and Artefacts*.

He recorded a talk for BBC-3, and was a guest on a television quiz.

'I knew you'd be all right,' said Anthony Finch. 'I've known all along that it would sort itself out. If there's anything I can ever do, you won't hesitate to ask, will you?'

Maggie suggested that he should move into her Putney flat. He said he would find somewhere else, and they could start off on the proper footing. And Maggie said, 'That's a pompous way of putting it,' and within range of her, warmed by her laughter, he found it impossible to argue. He moved into the flat, saying several times a day — perhaps once a day to Maggie and four or five times a day to himself — that he must find a place of his own, and then . . . And then and then and then.

It was all right. And it was a lot worse.

He was apparently not being pursued. There was no danger. He could settle down to work now. There was the book to be written, and another publisher wanted his help on a translation.

In London he saw more newspapers. Headlines and placards shouted at him. Few of them now concerned Czechoslovakia.

'Remember us when we are no longer news.' That had been a student's cry to reporters quitting Prague when it no longer merited the front page.

No longer news. From columns here and paragraphs there he deduced that the sequel had not been as bloody as everybody had predicted. There was still hope: less boisterous than before, but still hope.

In a way it was an anti-climax. He was horrified by a vision of his own selfishness. A part of him would almost have preferred news of total disaster in order to justify his own flight.

When he had been a visitor, choosing what he would see and hear, England was where he had claimed to feel most at home. Now he had chosen it as a refuge; and he felt utterly alien. Even when he was most ecstatically with Maggie, it was only a brief ecstasy. In a short time he was back in solitary confinement.

He would get used to it. He had to. Gradually he would adjust. He would do good work here, and he would make Maggie happy. That, at least, he had faith in.

The BBC asked him to contribute to a television symposium on student unrest. The Chairman threw him the lion's share of the debate. When a Conservative M.P. declared that what these long-haired demonstrators needed was two years' military service to knock some standards into their weak heads, Jan was encouraged by a skilful leading question to say that it was young people of this very type who had manned the barricades in

Prague and hurled defiance at the invaders.

'Not the same,' snapped the M.P. 'No comparison.'

'A very valid comparison,' interposed a sociologist who had allied himself with Jan from the start. 'Supposing similar circumstances in this country — '

'Ridiculous.'

'Supposing similar circumstances, it would be just these youngsters who'd stand up against tyranny.'

They argued with what Jan recognised as calculated acrimony. The Chairman knew his job. When things seemed to be getting noisily out of hand, they were in fact being held on a skilful rein.

At the end, the Chairman turned again to Jan. 'I wonder if you'd care to accompany our commentator on the Rhodesia House demonstration this coming Sunday? You might want to amplify your views, or comment on something from a quite different angle.'

After they had been released from the gaze of the cameras they were all given a drink. A crisp young blonde in a crisp primrose-yellow blouse and a mini-skirt arranged times and places for Jan on the Sunday, and suggested a fee. They all shook hands all round, and went their separate ways.

Jan didn't think the televised argument had established anything one way or the other, and couldn't imagine that his contribution to Sunday's programme would be of any greater significance.

Maggie had been watching the screen at home. When he reached the flat he found her talking to a man with emphatic eyebrows and a craggy nose.

'Arnold Westwood . . . Jan Melisek.'

Again a meaningless shaking of hands. Arnold Westwood said: 'An impressive performance, Professor. It *is* Professor, isn't it?'

'We thought you came over marvellously,' said Maggie. 'Of course, that ass from silly Sussex — '

'I'm glad you see through all the apparently unco-ordinated violence to the truth beneath,' said Arnold. 'I thought your comparison a most moving one. I doubt whether most people have given it a thought — least of all the ones who make the loudest noises.'

'So you're off to the Rhodesia rally on Sunday,' said Maggie. 'Arnold here's one of the organisers.'

'If there's anything I can tell you beforehand . . . '

The lights in the studio had given Jan a headache. They went on talking and he must have contributed his share automatically, but he was glad when Arnold got up to leave. Then, and only then, there was an awkward pause. Arnold looked at Jan and at Maggie. An adolescent moodiness shadowed the corners of his mouth. Jan wondered if it would be tactful to pretend that he, too, was preparing to leave. He stayed where he was.

At the door, Arnold said: 'Things in your home town haven't been quite such a carve-up after all, I see.'

Jan was sure it hadn't been meant as a jibe. But Maggie glared at Arnold, and Arnold flushed and looked sullenly back at her.

Sunday was warm but overcast. Trafalgar Square was inundated by a gently bobbing, swaying tide of young people. Jan was impressed by the orderliness of the crowd and by the sheer size of it. Demonstrations in Prague had been sporadic, consisting mainly of small groups making angry sorties and then vanishing. At most there had been a hundred or so at one time, and more often they could have been reckoned in scores. Here there were thousands. But Prague had been real and deadly. How real was all this?

Faces turned upwards as a loudspeaker began to thunder. Dusky smears of darker features dappled the surface.

Police stood at ease on the perimeter, and discreetly far back was a row of mounted policemen.

A speaker raised a clenched fist above a microphone and harangued the crowd. They took it calmly. When he spoke of sentences without trial, there was a faint murmur of agreement. 'Independence?' cried the speaker. A swirl of pigeons took off over the rooftops. 'Independence from what — from law, justice, reason, humanity?' A deeper roar swelled up.

Sentence without trial, remoteness from law . . . they were just learning, just discovering anger and the frustration of action. England was indeed far, far off the coast of Europe.

The man with a hand-held camera stood beside him. The commentator said: 'That's rather a dolly over there. Let's dig out some of her philosophy.'

The two of them advanced, and were back in thirty seconds.

Jan said: 'You're not transmitting all of this?'

'Heavens, no. Highlights early this evening, maybe an amplified version later. Depends how rowdy it gets.'

As the voices boomed on, the camera was turned on Jan and he answered a few off-the-cuff questions. 'Just to keep the record straight,' said the commentator. Jan had a feeling most of it would be eliminated before the public saw it.

A scuffle broke out on a far corner of the crowd. Someone began to shout. A rhythmic chanting began. An olive-skinned young man with a drooping moustache sprang up and seized a microphone. There was a discord of yelling.

Suddenly, as though shoved violently from the side, the crowd surged across the square. The television truck accelerated, nudging its way along the flank. The man with the hand-held camera plunged into the middle of the flow, and the commentator caught Jan's arm. 'If we try to stand over here . . . no, see if we can get the mike over this side . . . '

The crowd was transforming itself in a matter of seconds into a mob. It raced towards the Strand. Half a dozen mounted policemen kneed their horses forward as though to form a bank against which the wave would break. Jan was caught up in a current which swept him away from the commentator and past the railway station. He tried to break out towards the pavement and the shop fronts, but was carried along.

Somebody grabbed his arm and threw him to one side. A gap opened in the fringe of the mob, and he found himself teetering above a steep flight of steps. At the bottom, in a quiet street, a young

Negro was punching desperately back at two hulking white men.

Jan steadied himself against the wall. His hand was brutally knocked away and he was kicked on the ankle. As he fell he tried to go slack, letting himself crumple down three or four steps before jarring to a halt.

A man leaped after him. A foot in midair, a distorted face that nightmarishly didn't belong here but surely in Prague? A face seen across a street, in a queue . . .

He seemed to have all the time in the world to wonder where he was going to be hit and how much it would hurt. He took the shock of the impact against his right shoulder and then there was somebody else charging down the steps, and three of them rolled down. Jan lashed out, came to a stop again. He tried to get up, but a pain in his stomach doubled him up. Winded, he propped himself against the wall. Somebody was lurching away down the steps and out over the street below, past the battered young Negro.

Arnold Westwood said: 'You all right?'

'You got here quickly.' Jan was aware for the first time that his lower lip was gashed and starting to swell up.

'Sorry,' said Arnold. 'Sorry.' Jan couldn't see why apologies were called for. 'I didn't believe Maggie. Thought she was exaggerating.'

'Exaggerating?'

'While we were watching you on telly the other night. She said you were telling them where you'd be today, and someone'd be bound to take a crack at you.'

'So. She did?'

'Glad I was close when it started.'

A thickset man clattered down the steps.

'Professor . . . sorry, sir.' Apologies were flying as thickly as the clamorous abuse in the Strand above. 'Did try to keep tabs on you, but lost you in the crowd. Got a bit churned up, up there.'

*　*　*

Gould appeared at the flat next day, after Maggie had gone to the Chinnery office. 'Sorry about that.' He added his penitential mite. 'We did try to keep an eye on you. We had a hunch someone would try something.'

'You've been having me watched?'

'Can't keep it up indefinitely, I'm afraid.'

'I didn't ask — '

'No, I know you didn't. Just that we were . . . curious. We still haven't satisfied our curiosity.' Gould produced the map. As he handed it to Jan, he said: 'Nothing. Not a trace. No microdots, no clever squiggles, no watermark stunts. Nothing.'

Jan held the paper between his hands. Then he slowly tore it across, folded the pieces and tore again.

'Wait!' Gould reached out instinctively.

Jan went on tearing. 'I know it by heart. I don't need to carry it with me any longer.'

'You might need it as . . . well, a bargaining counter.'

'No bargains,' said Jan. 'Not for me.'

For once Gould seemed at a loss. He ventured: 'If somebody does approach you — '

'It will not be here,' said Jan. 'I'm sorry to have been a nuisance to you, but it won't be long now. If there are any more complications, they won't be on your territory.' He dropped the fragments of the map into the waste-paper basket. 'I am going back.'

'You don't mean back to Prague?'

'Yes.'

'But . . . after all this trouble? All the trouble you took to get here? I mean, now it's all right — now you know you can settle down here — it's still a whole lot safer here than it is over there. You've said yourself, there's bound to be somebody waiting for you at the other end.'

'It is now I know I am all right here,' said Jan, 'that I know I must go back.'

'Even though they'll be waiting?'

'I will never find the answer to the problem over here.'

'The map, you mean?'

'That. And other things.'

'But — '

'In my work, I have always to be stubborn. That is what it is, ninety per cent of it: stubbornness. To go on and on and on, until you find the shreds of truth in the mountains of dirt — and fit them together.'

He thought of Maggie coming home that evening, and wondered how he was going to tell her.

13

To hell with them all. With Mrs Chinnery and Mummy and Arnold and her job and everything else. To hell with the lot, said Maggie aggressively to herself as she waited in the departure lounge, bludgeoning down the awareness that she was well on the way round the bend and probably scaring the daylights out of people who depended on her in one way and another.

She had bought her duty-free bottle and was scanning the perfume list when Jan spotted her. She saw him from the corner of her eye as he stood quite still, then paced incredulously towards her.

'You said you would not come to the airport to say goodbye.'

'That's right,' said Maggie.

'And' — he gestured across the lounge — 'only passengers are supposed to be in here.'

'That's right. I'm a passenger.'

'No.'

'To Prague.'

'No,' said Jan. 'No, it's impossible. I should have guessed. But no.'

'You can't stop me,' said Maggie. 'I'm a free-born British subject, I have a passport full of promises of protection, and I have a valid visa. If I say I'm going to Prague, I mean I'm going to Prague.'

He caught her right hand between his two warm palms. 'Please, Maggie. My dearest, please don't do anything silly. Please go — go back home. When I can come back — '

'*If* you come back,' she said. It sounded brash and stupid, and she knew she was raising her voice in the same loud denial of common sense. 'I don't trust you,' she laughed shakily. People in the lounge looked round. 'You wouldn't come back, ever.'

'Maggie, please . . . '

The electronic chime heralded the announcement of their flight departure. Maggie picked up her grab-bag, waved it under Jan's nose, and turned towards the exit channel.

The plane was less than a third full.

She and Jan sat well forward. Outside, a dank mist threatened autumn. The plane howled up at a steep angle in search of sunshine.

When they had unfastened their seat belts, Jan said: 'Now. In Prague, you will stay away from me.'

'Not a very loving remark.'

'You understand me. At the airport I go through alone. If there is to be an incident, you are to keep clear of it. Probably there'll be nothing. I will go back to my flat, and when I think there is no risk I will get in touch with you at your hotel.'

'And what do I do while I'm waiting?'

'You can occupy yourself,' said Jan drily, 'with whatever business is the excuse for your travelling to Prague.'

He looked away, presenting her with a reproving profile. She wanted to reach out and touch him, to make him respond. She wasn't going to let him shut himself off from her. He wasn't going to go grimly back into captivity. Because that was what it had been, she knew: captivity.

Stubborn, she raged within. Proud,

stubborn, pedantic . . .

Her hand was clenched on her knee. Without looking at her he insinuated his fingers between hers and gently forced them apart.

Cloud built up below them. A grubby blanket lay over Europe, as far as the eye could see.

They had been flying for over an hour when a voice crackled through the cabin.

'This is your captain speaking. There is fog at Prague. Conditions have been deteriorating rapidly, and I am afraid we shall have to divert to Vienna. As soon as the weather improves, it is hoped . . . '

'Vienna?' Jan groaned.

'You think it really *is* fog, and not . . . well . . . ?'

At Vienna they were offered a meal. No promises could be made regarding the flight on to Prague. There would be an announcement an hour from now.

Then another hour from now.

Arrangements could be made for passengers to go on by train.

Maggie said: 'Oh. That means they're expecting the fog to persist. They don't offer you a train unless they're desperate: it's bad for the image.'

'So we sit here.'

'Or hire a car,' said Maggie. She leaned towards him. 'Jan, if anyone's waiting for you, they won't be expecting you by road. Even if they hear about us landing in Vienna, they can't check every frontier crossing — trains, cars, the lot — can they?'

'We will hire a car,' said Jan.

He had brought English money with him: his television fees and part of the advance from his publisher. Nobody had asked him about it at the airport. Nobody had asked Maggie, either, but she had law-abidingly brought only her strict entitlement.

It took forty minutes of negotiation to hire a car, and Jan had to put down a large deposit. Maggie was absurdly pleased by this, as though it constituted a cast-iron safeguard: Jan would have to bring the car out again to get his money back. They would come out again. Together, she vowed.

They drove back towards that frontier

they had crossed a lifetime ago.

The afternoon was gloomy. There was not a breath of wind. Haze like dirty water filled the valleys, and wisps of murky cloud clung to the treetops.

'It has been a melancholy summer,' said Jan abstractedly.

No Russian guards were visible at the crossing point, but as they moved on into Bohemia there were huddles of steel and dark uniforms in the woods. The tanks and guns had been drawn back into obscurity. It was impossible to see whether they faced the border or whether they were turned threateningly inwards.

At a crossroads, Jan slowed. There were still no signposts, but he said: 'Ahead, we come to Prague. If we turn left here, we can go through Sumava.'

The name meant nothing for a moment. Then Maggie remembered. 'Your map. This was where your friend came.'

'And where I came — with no result.'

'This time,' she said. 'This time, perhaps . . . '

'Before I risk Prague,' he said, 'let me

have one more try. Here, just once more.'

Maggie was thrust back against the seat as he turned, accelerated and raced along a road which had been ruined by neglect, weather and tank tracks.

They bounced and jolted along a valley and through a forest. Broken branches had fallen across the road here and there. There was a flicker of colour through one avenue of tree trunks, and in a clearing she could just discern a cluster of tents. Remembering last time, she waited for a tank to sway out on to the road here, or a hundred yards farther on, or somewhere on the next meandering mile. But Jan wrenched the car round a corner, and there was nothing ahead; and another corner, and still there was nothing.

The sky darkened and seemed to sag down on the black pinnacles of the forest. The windows of the occasional cottage or farmhouse gave out no light, and nothing stirred.

Jan flicked the headlights on. The bright swathe cut through ruts and coppices, and bounced over sudden swerves in the road. Maggie's eyes ached.

She closed them, but was being too erratically jolted from side to side to be able to relax.

She had no idea how long it took them, but at last she felt the car slowing and opened her eyes, and saw the lights sweep across a wooden fence and come to rest on the varnished log frontage of a small hotel.

The middle-aged woman who came to meet them peered dubiously at Jan, then seemed to recognise him. They shook hands, he said something, she came out with a spate of words and kept talking while she shook hands with Maggie.

As they went indoors, Jan said: 'She remembers my last visit. They are delighted to see anybody now — anybody they have seen before. It seems to stabilise things.'

'I can imagine,' said Maggie. 'Yes, I can guess what it feels like.'

'And her son is back. She's happy in spite of everything that's happened, because her son has come home from Prague at last — and with a wife!'

'Back to the old homestead,' said

Maggie. 'Not a bad idea, when things get too rough in the city.'

She didn't know what Jan explained to Mrs Rakovec, or whether indeed he bothered to explain at all; but they were put into a large old room with a perilously sloping floor and a large, ancient bed.

'Tomorrow,' said Maggie, standing at the window and peering out into an impenetrable wall of trees, 'we solve your little mystery once and for all. Right?'

'Tomorrow.' Jan nodded thoughtfully.

She found it hard to believe they were here. It was so still, so remote. They had fled so precipitously, and come back so easily. All too easily. A let-down, really.

In his arms, she murmured: 'And when it's settled, you really will write it off, won't you, Jan? Draw a line and say that's that and start again. Write it off . . . and come away again?'

He kissed her where, only a few minutes ago, he had avidly bitten her. 'Dearest Maggie,' he said.

It was no answer, and despairingly she knew it wasn't meant to be.

They set out early from the hospoda. 'We start,' said Jan, 'where I left off last time.'

It did not seem far. They skirted a village, passed a line of men working in the fields, and suspected the existence of a Russian contingent in one gloomy promontory of woodland.

'The border country must be alive with them,' Jan commented.

'Haven't they got a home of their own?'

'Probably not.'

He drove down a lane which petered out into dust and grit in a shallow valley. When they got out of the car, it was to inhale a steamy, rank smell.

Jan walked a few steps on. Beyond him, the flat expanse was broken only by tufts of spiky grass and an occasional velvety hillock. He slowed, and began to test the ground an inch at a time. At last his right foot pressed gently down and sank slightly. When he drew it back there was a plop.

Maggie joined him.

'Be careful,' he warned. 'Keep along this line.'

For an hour he paced to and fro. Sometimes he gave the impression of walking simply for the sake of walking, while he thought about something else; then he would grow more purposeful and there would be a calculated sequence in his movements.

Abruptly he turned to face out across the spongier part of the bog. He tested an edge with his foot.

On the far side, two men were digging. Perhaps digging peat for their fires, thought Maggie vaguely. But did they need to, with all this wood everywhere?

One of them straightened up, saw Jan, and shouted. Jan waved back. The man made obvious shoo-ing motions, urging him to retreat. Jan gave another reassuring wave and shuffled sideways like a swimmer nerving himself to dive off the edge of the pool.

He stopped. One foot went forward to test the ground. Another shuffle to the side, and another probe. And again. And again.

Then his foot did not sink into the softness. He edged forward, and the ground was still solid. 'Those lines between the shapes,' he said over his shoulder to Maggie: 'those divisions on Lada's map could have been indications of solid paths between . . . well, whatever those shapes are.' He advanced cautiously, testing every step. Then he tried a divergence to the left. His foot sank, and he had to draw it out with a lingering squelch.

It took ten minutes to find a transverse path, and it proved to be far from straight. Maggie, without realising it, had been breathing in quick, shallow gulps, and now felt dizzy. She called: 'Jan, it might give out. Or your weight might be too much.'

One of the men from the far side of the bog began to walk round, his spade over his shoulder.

Jan went down on his knees and reached out to pat and prod the unstable surface. At last, when his arm was grey with mud and festooned with grass and reeds, he gave up and made his way back as carefully as he had gone.

'There could be *something*,' he said. 'It

thickens very quickly. On the edges here it's not much more than a sludge on top of the earth.'

He looked round. At the foot of the slope was a long, whitened branch which must have fallen long ago from the trees above. He picked it up and leaned on it to test its strength. Then he groped out across the morass once more, still taking no chances. Balanced on the firm strip, he leaned out and forced the branch into the quag.

The man with the spade arrived. He growled something at Maggie. 'Pardon, anglicky,' she said. He looked startled, growled again, and then shouted at Jan. Jan rested on his branch and shouted back. There was a sibilant exchange, then Jan took some money from his pocket. Maggie could see that they were English pound notes he was waving.

The man, guided by Jan, began to wobble out towards him. The other labourer abandoned work on the far side and came hurrying round.

At the same time there was the sound of a car on the lane above. Its tyres scrabbled down the hill, and it stopped close to their hired car. A man in a sagging suit, his trousers shadowed by only the faintest memory of a crease, came towards Maggie.

She looked at him. He didn't seem very menacing, but he was obviously going to ask a lot of questions. Then she looked back at Jan, who was driving down with the branch once more. It stuck. The man with the spade braced himself and added his weight. The branch was forced slowly round like a paddle through treacle. Then it stopped. There was a consultation.

A voice spoke on Maggie's left. The newcomer was even seedier at close quarters, but there was something rather endearing in his self-deprecatory smile and in his tone of voice, even though the words meant nothing.

Maggie trotted it out again: 'Pardon, anglicky.'

He looked as surprised as his predecessor.

The second man with the spade puffed up. With much shouting and pointing he was guided out along the latticework of ridges. At one stage he strayed, and was in well above his ankle before managing to jab his spade obliquely into firmer ground.

The three of them went on their knees above the quag. Jan might almost have been preparing to thrust away from safety in a long crawl stroke. Lost in earth, their arms appeared to have been chopped off at the shoulders.

They braced themselves, and heaved.

A few murky, gaseous bubbles plopped on the surface.

Jan snapped an order. The three of them tensed and strained again.

The sour green crust opened in a sticky gash, as though in a primeval birth pang. The men struggled above it, and began to drag out a huge, limp placenta.

But it was no birth. This was a corpse. The head lolled, slime hung like glutinous cobwebs from the shoulders and forearms. The three men held it steady for a moment, then with a final heave managed to get it across the ridge and let it slump on to solid earth.

One of the labourers turned away and was sick.

Jan got up. He grasped the branch with

which he had started, and led the way back to safety, prodding ahead of him like a blind man.

Maggie said, in little more than a croak: 'Your burial ground?'

'It would seem so. I don't know how many more there are down there.'

'Not Celtic?' she said.

'No. And not Slavonic. Much more recent. And very well preserved.'

From what she had glimpsed, Maggie wouldn't have called the remains well preserved. She supposed that to an expert such things were relative.

'Quite modern,' Jan was saying. 'Quite a modern charnel-house.'

The man who had been standing a few feet back from Maggie now came forward. The hazed sun, shimmering through the dampness above the hills, struck a spark of light from the pens clipped into his breast pocket. There seemed, too, to be another spark: a flash of recognition, or semi-recognition, between him and Jan. They both nodded, spoke at the same time, floundered and then talked fast. The other two men joined in. Maggie looked from one face to another, and was none the wiser. Once again it was like being involved in a foreign film without sub-titles.

One man stabbed a thumb twice towards the farther slopes. The slopes, Maggie realised, which rose towards the border. She wondered if, at this very moment, field-glasses were being trained on them.

The man with the pens was holding forth at Jan. Jan snapped answers.

The corpse was a dripping huddle out on the bog.

Maggie cried: 'What *is* it? What's it all about?'

Jan smiled quickly at her, but only to keep her quiet. He went on talking. The other man spread his arms wide and began to speak more vehemently. Several times she thought she heard the name 'Rakovec'. But so many of the syllables were alike to her, so explosive and unintelligible.

They looked at the hills again. And suddenly she guessed, and said: 'Jan! Refugees!'

'Yes,' he said. 'That does seem most likely.'

★ ★ ★

The two men took their spades with them in the back of the reporter's car. Jan drove off in the lead.

'Yes, a reporter,' he said. 'We knew each other by sight, from the last time I was here. But I didn't know he was a reporter.'

'Didn't you say something about your friend having to *watch* a reporter here — find out about him?'

'Lada. Yes. If this is the same one . . . '

'What *is* it all about?'

Jan shook his head. Then, briskly, he summed up: 'Refugees from the old regime — Novotny's time. Poor wretches. They thought they were being led to safety by someone who knew the safest route, and then they were killed, robbed and disposed of.'

Maggie shuddered. 'Couldn't it have been the secret police: the authorities?'

'The authorities wouldn't have concealed the bodies. They would have given them plenty of publicity, to deter anyone else who wished to make a run for it.' The sun dimmed as they skirted the village. There were no heavy clouds, but the sky itself seemed to thicken into impenetrable greyness. 'It was all too easy. Most of them carried as much money as they could lay hands on. Especially foreign currency — they would pay a fortune for it. So kill them, rob them, roll them into the mire.'

'Didn't anybody ever ask awkward questions?'

'Who would ask? Friends who had been told they were going wouldn't dare to say a word. When your friends left for the West, you hoped nobody would remember they had been your friends. It was only when the thaw came and ordinary people could make contact with the outside world that the questions began. In Moravia there was a prosecution pending just before the Russians came in. And I did hear of one on the South Bohemian border beyond Krumlov, not so far from here. Now there is *this* to report . . . '

'And our friend back there will make the headlines. The newspaperman, I mean.'

'He seems to have a poor opinion of the Rakovec son,' said Jan thoughtfully. 'He will not say so outright, but I fancy he is already making deductions about what we have discovered. There were stories about the Rakovec boy being a hero, taking people to safety and then having to disappear himself. Our friend's a bit sceptical. He claims to know many unsavoury things about Josef when he was younger — things his mother didn't know, or didn't want to know.'

'And now the boy's back: isn't that what she told you last night?'

'Not a boy any longer. Grown up and married. Mrs Rakovec has given the prodigal a big welcome. But our reporter has a nasty mind: he thinks they are here because things were getting too hot in Prague for certain elements. Everything is upside-down. For the time being, it's the bad ones who are having to hide away, not the good ones. How long that will last . . . who knows?'

They drew up in front of the hospoda. As they got out, the reporter's car slowed in beside them. He came round to Jan, and again Maggie was sure she heard the name 'Rakovec'.

A woman sauntered round the corner of the building. When she saw the reporter she glanced frostily away and quickened her pace towards the main door. The reporter jerked his head significantly at Jan.

Jan turned to look at the woman.

He said: 'Blanka . . . '

14

She had not seen him. Jan stared fixedly at the doorway through which she had gone, half willing it to dissolve into a dream. Then Maggie spoke. He didn't register the words, but the spell was broken. He went into the hospoda after Blanka, along the passage. She was just closing a door at the end. He put his weight against it and pushed.

Blanka said: 'I'm afraid this is a private room. You should have turned to the right along there.'

He emerged from the gloom of the passage into the light. Blanka gasped and backed away until she was almost against the crude but ornate porcelain-tiled stove in the far corner.

Jan kicked the door shut and said: 'Now.'

The room had a naïve folk-art tapestry rug and a large wooden sideboard painted bright blue, red and green. The chairs were daubed with similar bravado, and above the fireplace stood a row of blotchy pottery mugs and ornaments. On the wall behind Blanka was a framed photograph which might well have been of the young Rakovec. Jan did not attempt to look at it closely: he had already surmised what name the young man had adopted for his Prague incarnation.

'So you're a member of the family now?' he said. 'Without even the formality of a divorce?'

'Jan. I was told you had gone. You left the country.'

'I returned to deal with some unfinished business.'

'But *here* . . . Why here?'

He said: 'I might ask you the same question. Too many people in Prague after his blood?'

'This is Josef's home. He wanted me to meet his mother and father. He's been working hard, he needed a rest — '

'From his job? Do his mother and father know precisely what his job was?'

'Jan, I know you must hate him. And me.'

'You established that to your own satisfaction before I left,' he said wearily.

'Jan, I told you. I'd been doing all I could for you. And I went on doing it. Really I did. I said all along I wasn't going to have you . . . well . . . '

'Well?'

'Well . . . killed,' she said. 'I wasn't going to let him kill you.'

'So thoughtful.'

'Or tortured, or anything,' she insisted. 'Or even thrown into prison. It's true, Jan, really it is.'

'Conscience,' he queried, 'or squeamishness?'

'Can't you see how I've tried to make things easy for you? I never wanted it to get beastly.'

No, of course she didn't. It would have made her ill. She would have winced; and wept. He wondered how hard she winced when Veselka entertained her by beating her, degrading her — whatever it was that gave him his hold over her. At what stage did the pain or the ugly vision cease to be a stimulus and become too much of a bad thing?

She had drawn her hair back in an austere bun, and she was wearing a pseudo-peasant blouse, presumably to impress Veselka's parents. Rakovec's parents, he meant: but the man was still Veselka to him. The clean, bright simplicity of the dress made her look lovelier than ever. She had a virginal sensuality that hurt his guts. But he could not bear to look into her tainted eyes.

He said: 'Tell me one thing. Did you plant that bug in our flat?'

'Oh, you found that.'

'So you did know about it. You knew all along.'

'No,' she said, 'not all along. Only later.'

'You worked for him. You never gave up working for him.'

'Jan, I did. Truly I did. When I said I wouldn't have any more to do with him, I meant it. I mean, I tried to mean it.'

'You tried to get me to incriminate myself. Nice, fatal additions to the dossier. *Agent provocateur* . . . '

'No. Well, that is' — her inexplicably sly smile was an echo of the past, a familiar humble, falsely humble, gleefully ashamed look — 'not provoking in *that* sort of way.'

'He was listening to me — '

'Listening to *us*.'

'All right, to us. But only because of what I could be lured into saying.'

'No.' She was irritated that he should have missed the point. 'Don't you see, he was mad with jealousy. He thought he'd lost me. It was driving him crazy. He couldn't bear to let me go. He had to try and hold on, somehow.'

'You mean he hoped to hear something he could threaten you with? Blackmail you into going back. Blanka, if it was that . . . ' Then it dawned on him what she did mean. It was too warped, too slimy. But then, so was the corpse out on the quag. He said: 'Eavesdropping?'

Blanka coyly lowered her eyes.

Not letting go. Holding on — as a tormented listener. What sort of love, or obsession, was that? Half gloating, half in a lather of despair.

Blanka said: 'Why did you have to show up like this?'

'You can't seriously tell me that he'd

bug our flat simply in order to scratch his dirty little itch? Sitting at the other end waiting, night after night, working himself up into a — '

'No,' she said. 'Oh no, it all went on tape. Then he could play it back when he felt like it.' She took a step forward, reasserting her right to be here. 'He played it when he felt like it,' she taunted. 'The night I went back to him, he played it then. Played it for the two of us. You understand? Played it while we were — '

'Yes,' said Jan. 'Yes, all right. I understand.'

'Honestly, there wasn't much on the tape.' It was a pale reproach, implying that Jan ought to have been more entertaining. 'Until . . . ' She stopped.

'Until what?' When she stayed mute, he demanded: 'What was on that tape that was so special?'

'What do *you* know that's so special?' she retorted.

'That tape. Tell me.'

'I don't know. We were just playing it — he hadn't had time before the Russians came, because he'd been busy on . . . well . . . '

'I can imagine. He'd been notified they were coming, he'd got a great big welcome ready. Must have been rushed off his feet, poor man. No, it wasn't really the time for sitting with your feet up, playing aphrodisiac tape.'

'He was more interested in that one little bit,' she said pettishly, 'than all the rest. Jan, why did you come here, to Sumava, that time?'

'So that was it.' He was glad to have this, at any rate, tidied up in his mind. 'That was why he was so slow off the mark. He didn't hear about my trip until that night. You hadn't mentioned it to him?'

'He knew you were away. That was what made things easy for us. But I didn't go into details.'

'So when he did realise what I'd been digging for, he had to make a last-minute grab. And he missed me.'

'Jan, what was it really all about? What were you *digging* for, then, if that's the word?'

'That's the word all right,' he said grimly. 'You'd better come outside and hear how far we've got.'

In a pool of watery sunshine outside the entrance, Veselka was standing and arguing, snorting and laughing, trying to browbeat the reporter. This might once have been his home but he looked out of place now. He was an alley cat, not a farm cat.

Jan stood back to let Blanka go ahead of him.

Veselka swung towards her. 'There's more idle gossip here than in the Alcron lounge on a . . . '

His voice died away. He stared past her.

Jan said: 'You must have been desperate to think you'd be safe here. Nobody else you could trust? Or did you just want to make sure that nothing around the old homestead had been . . . disturbed?'

Mr Rakovec and his wife were there. Maggie, a few feet from the others, was lost and uncertain.

It was Veselka's mother who said: 'Professor, we have told you about our Josef, who has come back to us.'

'Strangely enough,' said Jan, 'I believe we have met before.' He turned to Blanka. 'Do you know what your protector's youthful memories of this district encompass?'

The older woman who worked in the hospoda came out, wiping her hands on her apron. The landlord and his wife, sensing the hostility in the air, looked perplexed.

Veselka came a few paces closer to Jan and, with his back to the others, said companionably: 'A surprise to see you here.'

'I'm sure it is.'

'When we last met, you and I were close to an agreement.'

'That's not the way I remember it.'

'I see no reason why we shouldn't continue our negotiations. You'll thank me, in the long run.'

'You think you'll be allowed a long run? You think you're in any position to make promises — or threats — now?'

'It is only a matter of time,' said Veselka. 'We shall soon be back in charge. I'm offering you a chance. You have come back: that will count in your favour.'

'You know why I've come back?'

'Josef,' said Mr Rakovec, 'what are these stories we are hearing?'

Veselka turned and looked at the reporter. Yes, thought Jan, the reporter was assuredly on Veselka's list, singled out for the purge when it came. 'What slander is it *this* time?' Yes, indeed: a personal nominee from a long way back. Veselka tried to take Jan's arm. 'We can't possibly talk here. Let's go inside.'

Mr Rakovec blocked the doorway. 'We must know.'

'Leave the boy alone,' cried his wife. 'I don't want to listen to a pack of lies. You always had it in for him, all of you.'

'What was your job in Prague, Josef?'

'I've told you as much as I'm allowed to.'

'You're on the run,' said the reporter. 'Even the S.T.B. drew the line at collaboration in a Russian takeover, eh? All except one little poisoned cell.'

'Don't talk too loud,' breathed Veselka. 'I've nothing to be ashamed of. But others might be listening. You might be sorry. The battle's not over yet, you know. Don't be too ready to celebrate.'

One of the labourers said: 'Now can we go down and look at that place — all of you have a good look?'

'What are we talking about?' asked Veselka.

'The bog,' said Jan. 'Didn't you know how conscientious Ladislav Adamec was? He couldn't spend every minute of his day collecting the information you'd ordered from him' — Veselka momentarily betrayed himself by a quick glance at the reporter — 'so what else do you imagine he did? What else would he do but the work he had ostensibly come here to do? He explored. And he stumbled on the one thing you really ought to have instructed him was out of bounds.'

Veselka looked from one face to another.

The older woman said suddenly: 'My Jirka. Is he one of them, down there?'

'What's everybody talking about?' asked Blanka.

'How many?' asked the reporter. 'How many did you murder, Josef?'

365

'I have warned you. Do not talk too loud.'

Jan said: 'Did the S.T.B. find out somehow and recruit you under duress? Or were you a willing volunteer?'

Veselka yelped a mirthless laugh. 'Listen to this trumped-up intellectual! Don't you recognise him? Just the type who got us into our present troubles. He undermines the authority of our leaders, slanders his betters, makes it necessary for the Russians to intervene . . . and then sneaks out of the country with valuables and secrets, feeding capitalist spies with information. And now he is sneaking back in again by the back door. Trying to terrorise those who know too much about him. A traitor, with his English whore.'

Maggie didn't understand a word, but she flinched as Veselka's vicious gaze swept across her.

Jan hit him hard and accurately under the nose. Veselka lurched to one side, his arm up to his mouth. Jan went after him. Veselka steadied himself and lashed out with his left hand. They went down together on the ground. A knee thumped sickeningly into Jan's groin. He rolled away, and Veselka kicked him twice, savagely, in the back. Jan threw himself farther on so that he could stumble to his feet.

Veselka snatched a spade from one of the nearby men and charged madly.

His father grabbed the haft of the spade and swung it towards him. Father and son went down in a heap, and the spade screeched across the ground.

The men stood above Veselka as he tried to rise.

The reporter said: 'Since we are speaking of traitors, what about the betrayal of the Hrych girl, all those years ago?'

'My boy was only a child,' Mrs Rakovec wailed. 'He couldn't have — '

'The girl, too. She was only a child. And what about old Kus's brother, who was going to be taken over into Austria? Is he down there?'

'My Jirka,' said the woman again.

Veselka said: 'I have no intention of standing here any longer listening — '

'Tell them to go,' said his mother.

'They must go away, all of them.'

Jan said to Blanka: 'It would be too much of a coincidence to suppose that your cousin Jarmila is one of those awaiting exhumation. But somewhere in a place like that, buried in some forest, she probably suffered the same fate. From someone like your — '

'We are leaving,' Veselka said to Blanka. 'It was a mistake to bring you here.'

'No,' said his father. 'You do not leave. Not until we have seen. We will all go.'

'You're all mad.' Veselka took Blanka's hand. It was a tight, possessive grip, not a loving one. He turned her towards the hospoda. 'We will take our things and go to the village.'

Mr Rakovec had once again taken up his position in the doorway. The two men with spades stood on either side of the path, this time holding them firmly so that they should not be snatched away.

Veselka urged Blanka away towards the end of the building.

The woman who stood there was holding a kitchen knife.

The men with spades began to close in on Veselka.

'No,' faltered Maggie. 'Jan, they can't. You can't let them.'

'All we're asking him to do,' said Jan, 'is come with us and watch while we dig up whatever else is there.'

Veselka's mother whimpered. Then screamed — a thin, meaningless, animal scream, a release of intolerable fear and tension. The older woman put an arm round her and led her indoors. They heard the reverberation of her cries from an inner room, a rasping in-out, in-out of breathy terror.

Mr Rakovec looked unhappily along the passage, then out at his son. With his drooping paunch and his raddled cheeks, blotched with drink and weather, he was a comic caricature of a man, yet had a formidable dignity.

'I must know,' he said. 'We must all be sure.'

The reporter drove Rakovec, his son, and Blanka. Jan and Maggie took the two labourers with them. They made their way back to the noxious edge of the quag.

One of the labourers edged his way out, still unsure of the treacherous path. The other held his spade over his shoulder like a weapon, not taking his eyes off Veselka.

Blanka said: 'I can't.' She was brimming with tears, shaking. 'No, I don't want to . . . I can't . . . '

The man on the path stooped over the hummock that had not been there until this morning. He got it over his shoulder and brought it back. Maggie forced herself not to look away. Mr Rakovec bent over the corpse and began to wipe off the slime from what was left of the face.

Blanka tore herself away from Veselka and went down on her knees to vomit.

'No,' said the reporter, staring down. 'Nobody we know.'

'But there are more,' said Jan, 'out there.'

'This is absurd,' said Veselka. 'You think we stand about for days while you play at archaeology, Professor? You are too fond of the dead. Too fond of trying to make the dead prove things.'

'Do you know where to dig?' asked the reporter.

'I think so.' The two men took their spades and made their way a bit more confidently along the established ridge. 'Two metres farther on,' said Jan. 'The transverse path is there. Try that corner: I think it'll work out.'

It took only twenty minutes to raise the second corpse. They carried it back and laid it on the grass.

This time Mr Rakovec said: 'The hand. The way it twists. I know that hand. Kus's brother, yes.'

They looked at Veselka.

He said: 'This still has nothing to do with me.'

'Then you'll have nothing to fear,' said the reporter, 'when we call in the police and have the whole area dug over.'

Blanka, ashen-faced, crept back to Veselka's side.

'They're wrong, aren't they? They must be. Mad.'

'Mad,' said Veselka.

His father stepped forward.

The movement might have been a signal. Inside Veselka something snapped. He grabbed Blanka's hand and dragged her after him, out across the bog.

Jan sprang after them.

Veselka was literally running across the surface of the spongey ground. Even hampered by Blanka, he was making better progress than Jan could hope to do. He veered and swerved with the instinctive assurance of a child who had played and explored here for years. His feet had forgotten nothing.

The two labourers were running round the edge, along the valley to firm ground. But they couldn't hope to intercept Veselka and Blanka.

Jan made his way cautiously back.

Maggie said: 'They'll never catch them.'

Already Veselka and Blanka had reached firmer turf. They began to run side by side towards the far slope.

'If we drive round the valley,' said the reporter, 'we can cut them off at the head of the slope.'

'Jan,' pleaded Maggie. 'What's the use? What good . . . how can it help now?'

'We'd better go and see,' he said flatly.

They followed the reporter and Mr

Rakovec in the Skoda that skidded and racketed from one side of the lumpy road to another. Once, Jan risked a glance back into the valley. He saw two dark shapes scrambling up the far side. The cars curled round in a long, uneven loop, and rushed on through the trees.

'Blanka,' said Jan aloud. 'He's got to let go of Blanka. She had nothing to do with *this*.'

The car ahead skidded dangerously on a corner, and then led the way out of the trees on to a long, clear stretch. The firs made a jagged stockade along the skyline.

Veselka and Blanka, going a lot slower now, were plodding up towards that dark barrier.

The reporter's car stopped. He was scrambling out as Jan reached him.

'Not up there!' He stared up the slope, waved, and shouted. 'Not there — don't go any *farther*!'

The slope levelled off towards the trees, and after one glance backwards Veselka began to run again, still holding on to Blanka. His head turned once, twice, insistently, as though urging her on.

'Don't they *realise*?' breathed the reporter. 'Don't they realise how close?'

'Close?' Jan realised, all at once, how far they had come round the valley — how far towards the frontier. 'Oh no,' he said. 'No!'

The two Russians who appeared from the forest did so without haste. From here they looked leisurely in their movements, and quite unalarming.

Veselka and Blanka did not slacken their pace. They went on running. Perhaps they had not even seen the drab figures emerging.

'Come back,' Jan heard himself yelling. 'Come back!'

One Russian casually unhitched his tommy-gun.

There was a sound like the shriek of a circular saw whirring into a tangle of nails — a rasp, a squawking echo off the forest, and then what sounded like a long, diminishing sigh across the valley.

Veselka and Blanka went on for a few paces as though unhurt, but even as they stumbled forward their bodies were jerking backwards. They fell in a heap, and then there was no movement at all.

Jan put out a hand, and Maggie came close so that he could steady himself against her.

Mr Rakovec got painfully out of the reporter's car. He stared for a long minute up the slope. Then he began to climb.

'Wait,' Jan called. 'Wait until . . .

Until what?

The innkeeper went on climbing. Jan gently brushed Maggie's hand away, and set off after him. The Russians stayed where they were, watchful yet somehow incurious.

Veselka's throat had been perforated by bullets so that the head was almost torn from the body. His father pulled his own shirt off and wrapped it tightly round the mess.

Blanka's left breast and stomach oozed blood in a wavering diagonal. Her face was distorted in a last rictus of outrage, but there was no mark on it.

The two men stooped and lifted their burdens. The Russians watched and made no move.

Unsteadily Jan started off down the slope. The innkeeper came after, sobbing with the effort and with a deeper, appalling pain.

At the bottom they stopped, a few yards from the cars, and risked a glance upwards. There was no sign of anyone or anything between the dark, tightly marshalled trees.

15

She pointed, ticked off numbers on her fingers, and sketched quantities in the air with her hands. They were interested to discover she was English, and did their best to help her through the tangle of mutual incomprehension.

'I'll learn,' she told Jan.

Brambory: potatoes. Mrkev: carrots.

In kilos and not in pounds. Crowns and hellers, not shillings and pence. All right, it's easy enough. In a few weeks it could become a matter of habit.

'I'm learning.'

The flat in Prague was tatty, though Jan assured her it was better than most. She supposed she could get used to it, if she had to. It was fun; though not such fun one early afternoon when the warmth ebbed away and she was chilled through and through.

'The heating must have gone off,' she said to Jan when he came in.

'It often does.'

To him it merited no more comment than that.

'Haven't you an electric fire, for emergencies?'

'No, we don't have them.'

She didn't know whether he meant there was none in the flat or whether they didn't exist in this country.

She would learn, if she had to. Really she hoped they would leave before she needed to learn too much.

Jan was staying for the inquiry into the findings in the Sumava bog and the deaths of his wife and Veselka. Also, as soon as he was known to be back in Prague, there had been a summons to attend a sitting of the rehabilitation committee of which he was still a member. The Russians might be in the woods and camped discreetly around the cities; but the promised reforms were going ahead.

They returned the hired car by means of one of Jan's colleagues who was going out on a thirty-day visa. It was a holiday from which, Jan knew, he had no intention of returning.

'Oughtn't we to go, too, while it's still easy?' Maggie urged.

Still easy, provided you obeyed the correct procedures and didn't make a dash for the barbed wire.

'I must get the inquiry over,' said Jan, 'and round off my job on the committee.'

'How long will that be?'

'As long as it takes,' he said.

At night he was more demanding than ever, and savage with it, as though to use up all the passion he owned, to be rid of it and to finish. They didn't laugh so much or talk as they had once done.

In the daytime she wrote letters and innumerable picture postcards, so many that in a way the pictures became more vivid than the realities of Prague which she saw every day. Shopping, she protracted her blunders because they filled in the time.

There was something she was carefully not saying and not thinking. Their implicit understanding was no understanding at all. Then one evening she pushed her plate aside and said:

'Jan, I want to know when we're leaving.'

'I don't know.'

'But there has to be a date. Some sort of date we're aiming at.' She watched him pour a glass of wine for her, his hand and wrist turning slowly so that she was acutely, hypnotically conscious of the motion and of him. 'Jan, you *are* coming back with me, aren't you?'

He said: 'It must be dull for you all day. Much more sensible if you went to London and waited for me.'

'For how long?'

'You keep asking,' he said with a spurt of asperity, 'how long this, how long that. I can't package up my time in that fashion.'

'I only want to know when we can go home.'

He sat back, the bottle still tilted in his hand. 'Home,' he said. She knew, fatally, what she had made him declare. 'Maggie, my dearest Maggie — this is my home.'

'Not any more.'

'More than ever.' Tenderly he looked at her across an infinity. 'Maggie, I shouldn't have kept you waiting here. I can't leave.'

'But there's nothing for you to do here. Not now.'

'There's too much. It'll never be finished. Veselka. Blanka.' He forced the names out. 'They weren't the nice, tidy end of something, you know. They are part of what went on for too long and is still going on. There are others. There'll be more of it.'

'All the more reason for leaving.'

'If we all leave . . . all of us, all those who are stupid enough and stubborn enough to believe we have something good to offer . . . *something* that's worth the effort . . . then who is left? Who's going to shore up the country in the years to come?'

'It's not so long since you decided to escape.'

'And I came back. And here I belong.'

'I came back with you,' said Maggie, 'and I'll stay with you.'

'No.'

'Yes. I'm learning, I've told you. A couple of years, and you won't know me from a Prague tram conductress. Maybe

I'll *be* a tram conductress.'

Jan put the bottle down on the table. It was a punctuation mark — a final, black full stop. 'You're too young.'

'Oh, my God. I'm all of twenty-five.'

'All of you, I mean. You English. Too young to be Europeans.'

'Of all the bloody pompous — '

'It'll take fifty years before you even begin. And then that will be only the first generation. For you — *you*, Maggie — oh, my love, it would be too difficult for you here.'

'It's been done,' she said. 'Girls during the war. Czech airmen, and the rest of it. Your own mother,' she blazed, 'came from Wales. Was it so awful for her?'

'It wasn't easy.'

'I'm not asking for it to be easy. I'll learn.'

'Yes, you would learn. But is it worth it?'

'Don't you think it'd be worth it?'

He seemed to be slumping in on himself. He sagged until his arms were between his knees, his hands clasped as though to throttle somebody, or some intolerable idea.

He said: 'For me, yes. And yet . . . no, perhaps not. I'd be hampered in everything I did by the thought of you. We don't know what will happen, or how we'll be asked to meet the future. If I have to wonder how you will suffer, what right I have to have you here at all . . . No,' he shouted suddenly. 'No, it won't work. It won't work. I know, and you don't.'

'You don't want me,' she said.

'If I come to London . . . if all goes well . . . '

'I want to stay here.' She tried to laugh, tried to make him hear her saying *To hell with all of them, to hell with the whole bloody lot* . . . 'This is where the action is,' she said brashly.

'Please?'

She was seeing him through the wrong end of a telescope. He had receded, been snatched away from her. He was a foreigner who hadn't got a clue about contemporary English. She translated:

'It's a phrase. A bit dated, but . . . well . . . '

' "Where the action is." Yes, I see. Yes, it is here, I think. And I must stay here with it.'

'That goes for me, too.'

'You must go home.'

'No,' said Maggie.

'Yes, my dearest,' he said.

* * *

Her mother said: 'Margaret, how could you? How could you rush off like that, and never a word?'

'I sent you at least a dozen postcards.'

'Oh, *those*,' said Mrs Armitage.

Mrs Chinnery airily talked down Maggie's brusque, defiant apologies. 'My dear, I've always been an advocate of follow-ups. Efficient follow-ups. Go back and hit 'em where you hurt 'em the last time. But prior consultation — yes?'

Arnold, seeing the light in her window as he passed one evening, came and rang the doorbell. Maggie waited for shrouded reproaches or a hint of 'I told you so', even though he had specifically told her nothing. Instead, he said:

'How bad are things over there? It's impossible to believe a word you read in our papers. They're all slanted.' Without waiting for an answer, he went on: 'We're having a demonstration next Sunday.'

'About what?'

'About the Americans provoking trouble by instigating manoeuvres in West Germany.'

'Are they?'

'They're planning to. How hypocritical can you get. Do you know — this is what's so monstrous — do you know the Americans knew all about the Russian invasion from the start? From *before* the start. It was all agreed.'

'Really?' said Maggie weakly.

'It's just beginning to leak out. The Americans don't want the balance of power disturbed, any more than the Russians do. It suits both of them to keep their own people in a dither, taxing them into submission in order to pay for what they call defence. They did a deal, the two of them. The Russians had let America get away with subsidising the Greek colonels: and in return, the Americans agreed that although they couldn't openly approve of the occupation of Czechoslovakia, they wouldn't take any action

— and they'd try to talk anybody else out of taking action.'

Maggie wondered if the Czechs knew this, if they cared, if it made any difference whatsoever to them.

'You see?' said Arnold.

'Yes, Arnold.' It was easier that way.

'And after all,' he said radiantly, 'what could be worse for American politics and American propaganda, and America's inflated war budget, than to see an independent Communist state that was democratic and happy and that actually worked? Oh, no. Let the Russians do the dirty work, and we're all comfortably and profitably back where we started.'

'Mm,' said Maggie. 'So you'll be marching on Sunday.'

'Sitting down,' Arnold corrected her, 'outside the American Embassy.'

'Not the Russian?'

'You can't blame the Russians,' said Arnold. 'At least you know where you are with the Russians. It's the . . . the downright hypocrisy of the Americans. That's what it is.'

He talked on fervently. It all seemed a

bit late to Maggie, a bit stale, but she thought how nice it was to be so sure of the things you wanted to be sure of.

She wondered if Jan would come to England again. If it had meant so much to him in the past, surely he must come again.

Arnold refilled his pipe. He took a long time, tinkling spent matches into the ashtray before he could sit in his favourite position and study Maggie through a satisfactory curl of smoke.

'Mags, when I've got all this business out of the way, perhaps you and I — '

'No,' she said.

'You haven't even let me finish.'

'I don't want to hear,' said Maggie. 'I don't want to hear promises about what's going to happen when this is all over, or that's all over, or those loose ends have been tidied up, or whatever.'

Arnold sucked at his pipe. 'Mags, love, you've been hurt.'

'It's not mortal.'

'If you want to talk it out of your system — '

'No,' said Maggie. She was in no mood

of self-pity. 'I don't want to talk about it. But don't worry. I'm all right. I don't regret it, not one minute of it.'

'That's fine, then. Fine.'

'It's just that . . . ' She slithered on a giddy edge for an instant, just as in a dream, just as in that dream long ago in Prague when she had slipped off a step and woken with her heart pounding, and next morning there had been that tank staring through the glass panels of the door, and tanks in every street, on and on, and all the rest of the waking nightmare. It surged up in her and out of her like a disgusted, withering, scornful belch she couldn't even bother to subdue: 'Dead! Everything here's so dead. Trivial, futile. Irrelevant. Nothing to do with anything real that's going on or is ever likely to go on. Nothing to do with anything real, anywhere.'

'Yes,' said Arnold, at a loss. 'No.' He stopped sucking at his pipe, and it went out. 'Well, yes,' he said. 'Yes, there you are.'

Yes. Here she was.

Other titles in the
Linford Mystery Library:

BACK TO THE LEGION

Gordon Landsborough

The Brotherhood of Tormented Men is comprised of individuals who were prisoners, tortured in the underground cells of secret police in a dozen Arab countries. On a mission, they have crossed continents to rendezvous in the middle of the Sahara. When a travel-stained group of ex-legionnaires comes upon them, that mission should spell death to the men of the Foreign Legion. But death comes to men who accept it, and these legionnaires are fighters who refuse to accept death . . .

ONLY THE RUTHLESS CAN PLAY

John Burke

In the city of London, the *Career Development Functions* rooms are situated on the tenth floor of International Synthetics. There, people undergo the 'Fifth Executive Course'. The participants expect a gruelling challenge — one in which men fight for power — knowing that the going will be tough. But they don't expect one of their members to die in gruesome circumstances. So, is this a test of their reactions — or the insane ambitions of one of their own number?

THE CLUE OF THE GREEN CANDLE

Gerald Verner

Living in the village of Long Dene, best-selling novelist Roger Tempest is assisted by his secretary, Isabel Warren. When he unexpectedly disappears, Private investigator Trevor Lowe is summoned. But eight days later, Tempest's body is found, dumped at a roadside. The police establish that it's murder and they suspect Richard, Tempest's impoverished brother and heir to his fortune. However, Lowe remains unconvinced — even when Richard escapes police custody and goes on the run. Then there is another murder . . .